KYLIE GILMORE

Copyright

Rev Me Up © 2015 by Kylie Gilmore

Excerpt from *An Ambitious Engagement* © 2015 by Kylie Gilmore

All rights reserved. No part of this publication may be reproduced, distributed, or transmitted in any form or by any means, including photocopying, recording, or other electronic or mechanical methods, without the prior written permission of the writer, except in the case of brief quotations embodied in critical reviews and certain other noncommercial uses permitted by copyright law.

First Edition: August 2015
Cover design by The Killion Group
Published by: Extra Fancy Books

ISBN-10: 1942238118
ISBN-13: 978-1-942238-11-9

To the odd and unique in roadside America…

CHAPTER ONE

Nico Marino was about to get lucky. At work too. He was the boss, so he could take a fuck break whenever he wanted. He washed his grease-covered hands in the sink in the back of the auto repair shop and considered if maybe he should leave a little dirt behind. The red-haired beauty his stepbrother Luke was sending his way was a rich Manhattan socialite, who wanted a man who "got his hands dirty for a living." Another reason she'd wanted to see him at work, in his element so to speak. She'd seen a picture of him and Luke in front of Nico's prize 1971 Porsche 911E in Luke's Manhattan office. She'd asked Luke to arrange the meeting to indulge her blue-collar sexual fantasy, though she'd couched the request more subtly. Nico was happy to oblige.

He dried his hands on a paper towel and headed to his office in the back the Exotic and Classic Restorations showroom. Nico owned the shop, which consisted of a showroom, lot, and four-bay garage for the restoration work. Unfortunately, he didn't fully own the shop. He took it over from his former boss, Kevin Mallory, when Kevin retired four years ago. Nico paid him a stake up front, but, despite saving like crazy, buying out his silent partner was going excruciatingly slow. Nico liked fast in everything—cars, women, making money. He was thirty-two and it was way past time for him to make something of himself. To be a success. He was always on the hunt for a prize barn find, some undiscovered beauty of an old car to restore and sell for the big bucks.

He took off his work shirt, hanging it on a hook on the back of the office door, and sat at his desk in his clean white undershirt. He figured the woman might want dirty hands, but she wouldn't want grease on her fancy designer clothes. He had twenty minutes to kill before she got here, so he went through some of the paperwork cluttering his desk. Only five minutes later, the front door of the showroom chimed. He glanced over through the one-way glass window facing the showroom and caught a glimpse of red hair. She was early, but what the hell. He cleared the desk of paperwork and stacked it in a pile. Now he had two surfaces to work with—wall or desk, depending on which way things went.

He stood and watched the red-haired beauty for a

moment. She took off her large round sunglasses and tucked them into her purse, looking all around the place. She looked younger than Luke had described. Probably had plastic surgery like all the wealthy society women. She wore a dark blue sleeveless dress with yellow flowers that showed off an abundance of curves in all the right places. Her feet were in green spiked heels with a bow across the front. The bow with its girliness was a sharp contrast to the spiked heels, which sent a very different message.

Intrigued, he made a quick exit from the office and strode across the showroom. As he approached, she looked behind her and then back to him. She was tall for a woman and, with the heels, they were eye to eye. He offered a hand with his trademark killer smile— part player, part charm. "Hi, I'm Nico."

She shook his hand. "H-hi."

She was playing shy. How cute.

"Right this way," he said.

He led her to his office and shut the door. "We both know why you're here," he said before he bent her over his arm and kissed her just like he'd seen in a movie once. She tasted like cherries, and he was unexpectedly greedy for more. The kiss went on and on, an urgency he hadn't felt in a very long time driving him. She was all softness, hot and sweet. Long moments later, he finally let her back up, breathing hard. Her bright blue eyes were wide.

And then she slapped him.

Ow. He put a hand to his stinging cheek.

"Do that again," she said.

He did, this time pressing her curvy body fully against him. Her tongue slid alongside his, which made him crazed. He couldn't stop kissing her, and the urgency to have her had him lowering her over the desk. He reached down and hiked up her dress. She squeaked.

He tore his mouth from hers. "What's wrong?"

She smoothed her hair. Her cheeks were pink. "If that's how you treat all your customers, I'll shop here more often."

Shop? Oh, fuck no. He eased himself off her. "Wait, who are you?"

She sat up. "Lily Spencer. My father has an account here. He told me to get whatever I want as a graduation present."

No, *hell* no. What had he done? Her dad, George Spencer, was his best, wealthiest client. He could barely think straight. All the blood had left his brain the minute her lips touched his.

His gut twisted as something truly horrifying occurred to him. "Please tell me you're not graduating high school."

She smiled mischievously and didn't answer.

"How old are you?" he barked.

"Relax. I just graduated law school."

He shoved both hands in his hair, trying to force his brain to think rationally while his body was still in full-tilt crazy lust. "So you're not Tiffany?"

She tilted her head. "Does Lily sound like Tiffany?"

"I thought you were someone else," he said.

"I'm not."

"Are you going to tell your dad?"

She gave him an impish smile. "Depends."

"On what?"

"On whether you do it again." Her cheeks were bright pink, and he didn't know if it was from their kiss or if she was blushing. Her voice came out soft. "That means I want you to."

He hesitated because this was so wrong, but he couldn't stop staring at her lush mouth.

And then she wrapped both arms around his neck, pressed her hot curvy body against his, and closed her eyes.

He couldn't help himself. He dove back in for more, one hand shoved in those silky locks, kissing her like a starving man. His other hand slid down her back to her ass, pressing her against him where he badly needed relief.

She pulled away a moment later, a bemused smile

on her lips. There was a small bow, a slight dip, on her upper lip that had him reaching out to touch with one finger, tracing it. She met his eyes with her electric blues, and he felt it like a jolt to his system.

She let out a shaky breath. "Maybe you should help me buy a car now."

He pressed his thumb to her plump lower lip, imagining that mouth on him. She was made for sin. "Yeah, sure," he managed. But all he could think was *more*.

She slipped past him and out of the office. He gave himself a moment to get rid of his massive hard-on, but it wasn't going away anytime soon. He pulled on his work shirt, buttoned it, and left it untucked, hoping that would give him some cover. Then he took a deep breath and joined Lily Spencer, daughter of his best client, in the showroom.

~ ~ ~

Lily was having a blast shopping for cars. The gorgeous amazing kisser, Nico, was falling all over himself to help her shop once he realized who her father was. Most car salesmen were not so accommodating in her limited experience buying her current car. He was seriously hot, like movie-star hot, and more than six foot, which was extremely important to her as a six-foot woman. Not to mention the muscular hard body he'd scandalously pressed against hers. Dark Italian good looks with olive skin, dark brown hair, deep brown eyes framed with long lashes, a stubbled jaw, and those lips. Holy kissable sweetness. Most gorgeous men completely ignored her. As he would once she made her purchase.

She couldn't believe she'd been brave enough to ask for a second (and third) kiss. For once, her impulsive nature trounced her usual lack of confidence around men. She had to really savor this time before he showed her the door.

"Show me again how the power window works," she said, secretly congratulating herself on wearing her contacts today. Luckily, the May weather had put her in a springy mood, so she'd worn her floral dress that covered some unwelcome poundage around her middle. The result of too many sugar-fueled nights studying. And years of being a chocoholic.

He obligingly raised the window up and down on a 1986 Corvette she had no intention of buying.

She tapped her finger against her lips. "I'm not sure. Let's keep looking."

He kept going, though she could tell he was getting tired of showing her every feature on every car. They'd been looking at cars together for an hour now. Still, she wasn't quite ready to leave yet. Law school had been such a long drudging haul of study, study,

study. She hadn't had sex in two years. Could she be blamed if she wanted to prolong this magical time with the most gorgeous man on the planet who'd kissed her just like she'd seen in a movie once?

She pointed to a cute maroon car. "Can I see the trunk on that one?"

He let out a breath of impatience and headed for the car, opening the trunk for her. She peered inside the large empty trunk. "Uh-huh." She headed for the front and peeked in the passenger-side window. "Stick shift. Too bad. I only drive automatic."

"It's a nineteen sixty-three Ferrari," he said through his teeth.

"So that means…?"

He clamped his jaw shut.

She was the first Spencer who almost didn't go to law school. The black sheep of the family and proud of it. She was also the son her dad never had. That's how he treated her, anyway, on account of her being an only child. Apparently, he'd really wanted a boy to carry on the family legacy. Her dad was rough and gruff, always trying to, as he said, "toughen you up for the real world." When she finally agreed to go to law school, he was thrilled, until she switched from corporate law to environmental law. Yup, she was a tree hugger. Which made her real popular with her family, who represented big oil.

A very glam, tight-skinned woman with dyed red hair came into the showroom and sashayed up to Nico. She looked to be in her forties with a spectacular boob job.

"You must be Nico," the woman said, running her hand up and down his chest. "I'm Tiffany, and I'm ready when you are." That last part came out in a throaty growl.

Nico stepped away and glanced at Lily. "I can't."

Tiffany's brows shot up, but her face barely moved. Botox. Lily had seen it before on plenty of women at the country club. "But Luke said—"

"There seems to be a misunderstanding," Nico said.

"Me," Lily said with a great deal of understated sympathy.

Tiffany turned and narrowed her eyes. "Who are you?"

Lily smiled sweetly. "I'm the woman who got here first." She ran her tongue slowly over her top lip. *Such the slutty vixen today!* "He was phenomenal."

The woman huffed and turned to Nico. "I'm supposed to be second course?" *Slap!*

Lily winced as Nico's other cheek now had a pink slap mark to match the small print from her hand.

He rubbed his cheek and glared at Lily.

The other woman stalked out of the showroom.

Lily shook her head. "Two slaps in one afternoon? That's gotta hurt."

He narrowed his bedroom eyes. "Why are you still here?"

"I need to buy a car," she explained patiently. She rubbed his arm, his firm muscle making her stomach flutter. "I should get some credit for not really meaning my slap. It was symbolic."

He cocked his head. "Oh, yeah? Cuz it felt real to me."

She shook her head. "Not like Tiffany's slap. She was really mad. I was just doing what any classy lady mauled by a strange man would do."

He scowled. "I didn't *maul* you. I kissed you."

"Mmm. It was a good kiss, wasn't it?" She still couldn't believe it had really happened. Her, practically virginal Lily Spencer, ravished by the stunning Italian sex god. She went hot all over just thinking about what almost happened. Right on his desk.

He scowled some more. She felt a tad remorseful for yanking his chain over the past hour. "I'll take the Tesla." Electric cars were better for the environment.

Nico advanced on her, and she stood her ground, hoping he might kiss her one last time before he got her dad's money. It was what most men wanted from her.

He glowered at her. "Did you see a Tesla in my showroom? Did you see anything that might have been as recent as that in my collection of *classic* cars?"

"No, but that's what I want."

"And you made me do all that demonstrating?" He gestured around the showroom. "Open the trunk, close the trunk, roll up the windows, roll down the windows, lock and unlock, look in the glove compartment. On all those cars that are clearly not Teslas?" His voice got really loud at the end there.

She shrugged daintily.

"Get out."

Her jaw dropped. "What?"

"I said get out."

"My dad gave me a blank check. You're just going to turn that away? Can't you special order it?"

"I don't like being messed with." He stormed out of the showroom and went to his office, where she'd had the best kiss of her entire life, and slammed the door.

CHAPTER TWO

"What the hell did you do to her?" Luke hollered. Nico pulled the phone away from his ear. Luke had called just as Nico was locking up work for the night.

"Nothing."

"Well, it must've been something. Tiffany fired me."

Nico shoved a hand in his hair. "Sorry."

"She had a lot of money to invest, so this better be a damn good explanation."

Nico jerked his chin at Brian, his best mechanic, as Brian left. He went into his office for privacy, shut the door, and sat at his desk, feet propped up on top. "Another redhead showed up."

A beat passed.

Luke snorted. "You didn't." His stepbrother was the same age as Nico, and they were close. They'd been each other's wingman when it came to women since high school. They were similar in height and build, but looked nothing alike—Luke had dirty blond hair, fair skin, and blue eyes while Nico was dark-haired Italian through and through. But they'd discovered their combination of looks and charm always worked on a group of women. They weren't competition so much as two very different options. Luke was all smooth talk; Nico was all disarming good humor.

"Yup," Nico said. "Got slapped once by the first redhead and then a second time by yours."

Luke barked out a laugh.

Nico reluctantly smiled. "She didn't want sloppy seconds."

"Did you really screw a customer?"

Nico put his feet back on the ground and sat up as a vision of Lily under him on this very desk—eyes wide, pink cheeked and breathing heavy—flooded his brain. That mouth. Those plump pink lips.

"Nic?"

Nico grabbed his keys and headed out, locking the door behind him. "It didn't get that far." He stepped outside. "She, uh…oh, shit, it was a disaster. She's the daughter of my richest client."

Luke let out a guffaw of laughter.

"It's not funny."

"Horndog ways catching up to you," Luke wheezed before another bout of laughter.

"Yeah. Don't send me any more women with blue-collar fantasies."

"I don't have to. You'll do anything that walks in the door."

"Shut up." He punched the button to end the call. He wasn't pissed so much that Luke had laughed. He was more pissed about him talking about Lily like that. It wasn't her fault she'd stepped into his lair. He ran a hand over his face. He'd really screwed up. If he lost his best client, the hard-ass George Spencer, bankruptcy was just around the corner. Should he call her dad and apologize? But what if Lily hadn't told him anything? That would just be outing himself for no good reason. What he really should do is call Lily and apologize, but he didn't have her number, and he didn't know where she lived.

When he got home, he looked her up online and didn't find a home address or phone number. Probably unlisted. Well, she had just graduated law school. She was probably at her dad's mansion until she moved wherever she had a job. There was nothing to do but wait and repent his playboy ways.

~ ~ ~

Lily returned home to Fieldridge and the large Tudor-style home she'd grown up in. She greeted their housekeeper, Anne, with a cheery hello. She didn't know the woman well. Her father went through multiple housekeepers a year because he had extremely high standards and a no-second-chances policy, which also explained why she'd had so many different nannies growing up. Today had turned out fabulous. What a kiss! She'd relive it for hours. Days. And, *ooh baby*, nights.

Except for the tiny fact that she'd managed to make Nico mad at the end there, it had been perfect. He was the most beautiful man she'd ever seen in real life, second only to her movie-star crush Chris Bowman from the Rubberman superhero movies. The way Nico had kissed her was thrillingly scandalous, all thrusting tongue and firm lips. And the way he pressed against her on his desk. Nothing like it had ever happened to her. No man she knew would've dared touch the Spencer heiress like that.

She headed toward the glass conservatory at the back of the house, where her dad liked to relax with the paper after his Friday afternoon golf outing. She planned to return to Nico's shop tomorrow with the excuse of an apology for wasting his time and a desperate hope that he'd kiss her again. She sighed dreamily, imagining it. He'd see her, his eyes would light up across the room, and he'd rush to take her in his arms. "Lily," he'd say in that deep, masculine, sexy voice, "kiss me." Or better yet. "On my desk. Now." A delicious thrill ran through her at the thought.

"Did you get a car?" her dad asked, startling her from her fantasy. He stood and gestured for her to take a seat in the hard, uncushioned teak chair next to him. He was dressed in what he considered casual evening wear—a sport coat with patches on the elbows, button-down shirt, tailored pants, and loafers. He was a large man, six foot four, solid, very dignified. His gray hair was neatly parted and perfectly smooth. He looked down his patrician nose at her, though she always told herself he wasn't trying to look contemptuous, he couldn't help it if he was tall with a patrician nose. He *had* to look down his nose at her from that height.

Lily's cheeks heated, thinking of what she got that was so much better than a car. She took the offered seat. "I haven't made a final decision. There were so many cars."

His lips pinched tightly together as they often did before he spoke. It wasn't just her. He spoke like he'd sucked a sour lemon to just about everyone, unless he was trying to broker a deal that required smooth persuasion, then he could smile, however insincerely.

He took his seat again and finally spoke. "Did you tell Nico who you were? He should be giving you the VIP treatment."

"Oh, he was," she said, unable to help her small

smile.

Her dad grunted. "He's the man I hired to restore your grandfather's Mustang."

She straightened. "He is?" She'd recently inherited her grandfather's house and old Mustang out in California.

"Yes. He'll be heading out next Saturday to retrieve it. Long before your trip, so you won't have to deal with the car at all. Then he'll handle the auction. Maybe I'll buy it if it's anything special."

Lily had a flight booked to Los Angeles in three weeks to go through her grandfather's things with a brief detour to Vegas to deal with something that had nagged at her for weeks now. It was her grandfather on her mother's side. Someone she'd never met. Neither had her dad, for that matter. But she'd wanted to go through any family mementos that might be stored in the house. She knew very little about her mom's side of the family.

"Have you started studying for the bar?" her dad asked.

The bar exam was at the end of July, and she wasn't ready to get back to studying so soon.

"I just graduated a week ago. I need to decompress." She stood and kissed his cheek, knowing it would fluster him enough to give her an escape. He was extremely uncomfortable with affection. "I'm going to help in the kitchen."

"We have staff for that, Lily. How many times must I say that?"

She laughed. "I like cooking." She headed out.

"Spencers don't cook."

She turned. "Spencers don't hug trees either, but look what happened!"

He took a deep breath, in through the nose, out through the mouth. "Kent is more than happy to take you on at his firm." Kent was one of her father's Yale law school buddies.

"I have a job."

His lips did that sour-lemon thing again. "I hope you'll change into something nicer for dinner. I invited the Wilsons."

"Thanks, Dad. I hope so too!"

She turned and made her escape, annoyed as usual by her dad. First of all, she was already wearing a dress, but the request meant he wanted her in something more formal. Second of all, the Wilsons were there for an alliance of families. It was like some old-fashioned matchmaking between her and her childhood friend Trevor. He'd kissed her once before they left for college, an obligatory kiss, both knowing their families wanted them together. That kiss had been so chaste it was like kissing her brother. He thought so too. He actually wiped his mouth after. Jerk.

Being the proud black sheep of her family, she wore a little black dress to dinner with a scandalously low cut in front to show off her best feature—her cleavage. Her shoes were high-heeled Louboutins with lace-up booties that resembled pink sneakers. Her father had conservative designer dresses tailored to her exact measurements stocked in her closet for all formal occasions such as these. She'd worn them exactly never.

"Hello," she called, crossing to greet their guests where they stood in the two-story foyer. She air kissed Mrs. Wilson on both cheeks as she knew she liked, kissed Mr. Wilson on the cheek, and turned to Trevor, wanting to hug her childhood friend, but knowing he wouldn't like it. When they were kids, he was more fun. They used to play hide-and-seek in all the secret passageways for the staff at the country club. He'd grown up into a carbon copy of his boring, stiff dad. In any case, he had a personal space bubble that he didn't like crossed as she'd finally realized after numerous events such as these when she'd tried to hug him, and he'd stood stiffly, arms at his sides. She smiled instead, and he air kissed near her ear.

"Nice dress," he whispered. He was a breast man, as every female at the club well knew. He wore a pink shirt with pink and green plaid pants. Quite hideous.

"Nice pants," she whispered back.

"Thank you," he replied stiffly. He could never tell if she was joking or not, as he'd once mentioned. At twenty-five, he was already deeply entrenched in his father's corporation and a big hit on the golf course. He'd had a golf instructor since he was seven.

They headed to the formal living room for cocktails, and Lily braced herself for a long, boring evening. Her father gave her a dark look and stared pointedly at her sneaker heels. Lily ignored it and sat on the sofa next to Mrs. Wilson, who smiled politely.

"How's the garden club?" Lily asked, knowing the question would give Mrs. Wilson plenty to say while the men talked business and golf.

The older woman beamed and launched into a long description of their new "sunny islands" program to freshen up the small islands of grass at intersections around town. Lily sipped her gin and tonic, making sure she threw in a few well-timed *mmm-hmms* while she mentally returned to her time with Nico today. The way he strode toward her in the showroom, all tall, muscular confidence. That delirious moment when he unexpectedly stopped in front of her, instead of some beautiful woman behind her, and introduced himself. His smile, that perfect white-toothed smile that lit up his face, yet still screamed alpha Italian male. She crossed her legs tightly over the throbbing. Just thinking about him got her worked up. Imagine what would've happened if she'd actually let him—

"Lily," her father barked.

"Huh? What?" She looked around the room at the curious faces.

"Trevor asked what are your plans for the summer," her dad said in his formal, rigid, I'm-about-to-lose-what-little-patience-I-have tone.

"Oh!" she exclaimed. "I have some time off before I start my new job. I'm working for the Earth Defense Group."

Mr. Wilson frowned. "We've had some dealings with that group."

Lily smiled serenely. "I'm sure you have." Mr. Wilson was CEO of a huge land development company. Developers and environmental advocates often battled it out over declining habitat, endangered species, and wetlands protection.

"I'm trying to get her into Kent's firm," her dad said, "but she's being stubborn about it."

She wouldn't last a day there, and she knew it. Kent's firm represented big agri-business. The kind of pesticide producers and genetically modified food companies that Lily was one hundred percent against. She tried to eat local, fresh organic food whenever possible. She'd toyed with the idea of going vegan, but she liked cheese a little too much. And steak. And chocolate soufflé. She really loved food.

The rest of the night passed much the same. Her dad tried multiple times to shame her into toeing the line. True to form, she clung to her black-sheep label. His frustration was evident. Hers was well hidden. She'd like, for once, to feel accepted just the way she was. She was her father's daughter biologically, but that seemed to be where the similarities ended. She knew why. She had too many of the undesirable traits of her mother. She was too excitable, too emotional, too outspoken, just too much everything. Her dad had spent a lifetime trying to straighten her out. She'd embraced the dark, rebel side as a teen and hadn't looked back.

The conversation washed over her at the formal dining room table as she slipped back to her Nico daydreaming. The way he'd dipped her over his strong arm. The heat of his body through the thin white T-shirt he wore, the sharp tang of oil and clean, masculine scent, maybe his deodorant, she didn't know, but it was so hot. Those deep brown eyes that seemed heated somehow, powered by hot-blooded Italian—

"Lily," her father snapped.

"Huh?"

He scowled. Her father didn't like when she used slang. "Yes?" she amended.

"Trevor asked you a question."

She turned to find Trevor smiling tightly at her from across the gleaming cherrywood table, holding a small black velvet box in his hand. *No, no, no.*

"Lily Spencer, will you do me the honor of becoming my wife?" Trevor asked, opening the box to reveal a huge round solitaire diamond ring. Flawless cut and color, probably two carats. Trevor would do it up right.

"Why?" she asked. If he secretly loved her, very secretly because she hadn't known, she'd be gentle in her rejection.

"Lily!" her dad scolded.

Mr. and Mrs. Wilson whispered something to each other.

"Because we get along well," Trevor said. "Our families could be good for each other. And I'm prepared to sign a prenup."

Everyone looked at her expectantly. Her trust fund was deeper than his, so she understood the prenup mention, her father would've insisted on it. Hell, she would've too after her disastrous engagement with John two years ago. Still, a marriage proposal without one mention of love was just wrong.

"No, thank you," she said.

Dead silence.

"Would you like more time to think about it?" Trevor asked politely, still holding the ring out to her.

She stood, knowing she couldn't prolong his agony. "I'm just not ready to settle down. Please save that lovely ring for a woman who truly deserves it."

She hurried from the room and headed upstairs, but not before she heard Trevor call, rather desperately it seemed, "I'll wait for you!"

What had her father promised him?

Lily paced her bedroom as the sound of angry voices carried upstairs. She had to get the hell out of Fieldridge soon. She'd planned on spending a few weeks back home before her trip to California, but now she was thinking sooner rather than later sounded pretty good. Things would be tense at home, and she worried that Trevor might think she was playing hard to get instead of impossible to get.

She got out her laptop and started looking up flights. Several minutes into her search, she leaned back and closed the laptop as an idea hit her that had her tingling all over. Why not go to California with the man who was driving to the same exact destination next week? That would accomplish two goals simultaneously. First, she'd get a chance to see America. A road trip was the ultimate summer experience—nothing but freedom and adventure. And she wouldn't completely blow off studying for the bar. She'd already downloaded all the audio lectures for an online bar exam review course. She could do that on the road through her iPhone easy peasy.

And the second goal she'd accomplish? Ending her dry spell. Hopefully. Her lack of experience was embarrassing. One man. She'd been with one man in twenty-five years. An unfortunate result of her Amazon size putting off most men in her social circles and her money attracting the wrong ones.

The Amazon-woman thing had been driven home to her early on at the exclusive prep school she'd attended. The popular girls were petite blonds with a pleasing, you're-a-male-so-that-makes-you-automatically-wonderful attitude. She was six foot (since ninth grade) and solid, as her very solid dad always said. Like a peasant, she always thought. Everything about her was too big—boobs, waist, hips. Her fat lips, ugh. Add in the red hair and snarky attitude, and that was the recipe for a virginal existence. In any case, her dad had forbidden her from dating in high school because he didn't want to deal with the worry of her getting knocked up. Or as he put it, "Causing a scandal that would mar the Spencer name forever." She would've snuck out of the house anyway if any guy had been interested.

By her senior year in high school everyone called her Slutty Spencer. She'd started the rumor. And she *still* didn't get laid.

Her experience hadn't improved at her Ivy League

college. She'd had to wait until law school. John had been her first. And last, unfortunately, because the way he'd dumped her in a clear case of wanting her money and not her had *hurt*. Like ego-crushing, self-esteem-destroying hurt.

Looking back, she supposed a twenty-two-year-old virgin with a trust fund was ripe picking. But, at the time, she'd been so thrilled to have the attention of a charming, smooth-talking cute guy with a sharp mind. He'd been a year ahead of her in law school. After one year and an engagement that ended when she told him about the prenup, John had been especially cruel when he'd informed her that he'd had to close his eyes and imagine someone hotter when they were in bed.

"It's like fucking Godzilla!" he'd yelled. "Why do you have to be so tall? Why can't you make any effort to be thin? I swear you weigh more than I do!"

She'd kneed him in the balls, but it was a small victory. She'd left his apartment and bawled her eyes out. All of her worst fears confirmed. She was too tall, too "solid," to ever be attractive to the opposite sex. She was Godzilla.

She'd been so devastated she'd gained twenty pounds in consolation chocolate. It wasn't just his cruel treatment. She'd felt close to him because he'd been her first, and the loss of that first close relationship was especially difficult because of her abandonment issues. Knowing you had issues and even talking about them in therapy still didn't make them go away completely. Later, she'd joined Weight Watchers and eventually lost the weight, but she'd gotten bored with all the calorie counting and settled back to her normal weight. Not huge, but not skinny either.

But that kiss with Nico had stirred up her long-deprived libido. Something about that kiss told her he might want to help her out. A road trip to California and a tutorial of sorts from the very experienced— woo! She got a hot flash just thinking about it.

But could she really go through with it?

She worried her bottom lip. If he turned her down, she could deal with that. She was used to not being the ideal woman in men's eyes. But what if he said yes? Could she push herself past all her Godzilla-sized insecurities and just go for it?

The front door slammed as the Wilsons left.

"Lily!" her dad bellowed. "I'm going out."

He'd likely go to the club, down a couple shots of rare Macallan scotch, and lament what a burden she was to the discreet bartender. She didn't answer. A moment later the house was quiet.

Was this really her future? A soulless, loveless marriage to a man who wiped his mouth after he kissed her?

That was it. She was going to California with Nico. She didn't care how difficult it was to get the words out. She'd do it and, somehow, she'd find a way to grab a hold of what she really wanted—passion, excitement, a great adventure.

She'd tell him in person tomorrow.

CHAPTER THREE

Lily returned to Exotic and Classic Restorations the very next morning as soon as Nico's shop opened. To apologize, of course. She really did owe him an apology for the way she made him show her all those cars for no good reason yesterday, completely wasting his time, just so she could be near him a little longer. She also had to let him know about their road trip.

Slutty vixen, slutty vixen, she chanted to herself in her own little motivational mantra. If she thought it enough times, maybe she'd come off that way.

She parked her cute cherry-red Prius outside next to a very sporty yellow race car and headed into the showroom. She wore contacts and another dress, a flowing sundress that emphasized her best features, boobs and legs. Hopefully that would distract him from what was in between.

Another sales guy was in the showroom.

"Is Nico here?" she asked.

The guy smirked. Nico probably had a lot of women show up looking for him. "Yeah, he's in the garage."

"Thank you." She went back outside and around to the repair shop with four open bays. It was Saturday and there were just two mechanics. She wandered in and found Nico bent under the hood of a car.

"Hi," she said softly so she wouldn't startle him.

He jolted and hit his head on the hood. He scowled at her, rubbing the back of his head. "I seem to get hurt a lot when you're around."

"I'm sorry. That's why I'm here, actually. To apologize for wasting your time yesterday with all those cars." He was still scowling, which reminded her that he wasn't entirely innocent in this scenario. "Even though *you* were the one who kissed *me* like an animal in your office." She glanced over to the door that might lead back to that den of delicious sin.

He immediately stopped scowling and looked contrite. "I'm sorry. I would've called you last night to apologize, but I didn't have your number. I thought you were someone else, but that's no excuse. I shouldn't have just—"

"You're forgiven."

"Did you tell your dad?"

"Why would I tell my dad?"

He nodded once. "Thank you."

He turned back to the engine he'd been working on. His hands were large and strong and covered in grease. His navy blue work shirt pulled tightly across a broad back and shoulders. How could she ever expect a man like that to give her a second look? He was one-hundred-percent hottie. And she was...not. Her fleeting confidence took a dive.

She turned to go.

"You still want the Tesla?" he asked.

She turned back. "No, that's okay. I've got my Prius."

"Then what'd you come here for in the first place?" he asked in a rather hostile tone. Like he wished she'd never walked in, so he wouldn't have mistakenly kissed her.

"I thought I'd take a look around," she huffed. "See if you had anything interesting."

"Yes, but you already knew you wanted the Tesla."

"I needed to get my dad off my back with an actual visit. He doesn't take no for an answer, as I'm sure you know."

He wiped his hands on a rag. "Yeah, I know."

"Anyway, I'm very sorry I wasted your time."

"That's all right. No harm done."

A surge of hope went through her. *Slutty vixen, slutty vixen.* "I heard my dad hired you to restore my grandfather's Mustang."

"Yup. I'm heading out there next weekend to pick it up."

"You want company?"

He raised a brow. "You want to drive to California with me?"

"With a brief stop in Vegas."

"Why?"

She shrugged, not quite ready to ask for a sex tutorial at this point in their relationship. And she definitely didn't want to get into the reason for Vegas.

"Freedom," she said simply. "Adventure." At his doubtful expression, she added, "I could really use a break between law school and being chained to a desk for the rest of my life."

"It's a work trip."

She flashed a brilliant smile, hoping it came across as flirtatious and encouraging. "Slash vacation."

"Why are you smiling like that?" His brows scrunched together. "I don't take vacations."

"Then you're overdue."

He shook his head. "I've got work to do."

She stopped smiling as he turned and went back to the car he'd been working on. And then it hit her that this was never going to work. He'd kissed her by mistake. He wasn't interested in her. She had nothing he wanted.

Or did she?

"Did you know the Mustang hasn't been driven since nineteen sixty-nine?" she called.

That got his attention. He crossed to her side, took her hand in his firm grip, and walked her out into the bright sunshine.

He stopped and leaned close, making her heart thump hard. "Tell me everything you know about that car."

It was so exciting to have him so close, she could barely focus on what she was saying. "I inherited my grandfather's old place in California. That's why I want to go out there, go through the stuff, pick out the family heirlooms. My mom didn't want any of it, so it's all mine."

"Lily, the car," he said.

She grinned and whispered dramatically, "Barn find." She watched the car shows with her dad sometimes when she was home on break. She knew the old untouched classic car left in someone's garage or barn was like the holy grail for car aficionados.

His deep brown eyes bored into hers. "What do you know? Your dad just said it was a sixty-nine."

She went hot all over. Except he looked so serious, she suddenly realized he meant the car. *Shut up, dirty mind.* She'd never done that number, but she'd imagined it quite vividly.

"My mom said my grandfather got it from a

neighbor," she said. "Some kind of limited edition deal, but the brakes didn't work when the other guy drove it to his daughter's wedding, so he put it in the garage and never drove it again. My grandfather intended to fix it, but he never got around to it."

"Whoa." Nico shoved a hand in his hair and staggered back. Wow. He seemed pretty excited. Almost as much as Lily was at the idea of a road trip with him. "Your dad never mentioned any of this."

"He doesn't talk to my mom. I do." Her dad barely spoke to his own daughter, either, but that was more family crap than Nico needed to know.

"How many miles on it? Is it...is it...a Ford Mustang Boss four twenty-nine?"

She shrugged. "We'll find out, right?"

"Do you have any idea how much an untouched nineteen sixty-nine Ford Mustang Boss four twenty-nine could go for?"

She shook her head.

He shoved both hands in his hair and pulled, making the corners of his eyes lift weirdly. "Who else knows about it?"

"Only my mom knows what I told you, but the house and all of its contents are legally mine. If you take me with you, I'll give you the car."

Nico started pacing back and forth.

"Are you okay?" she asked. He seemed agitated.

"How much you want for it?"

"You can have it just for the ride." And hopefully another kind of ride. Score one for slutty vixen!

His eyes narrowed. "Your dad wanted me to restore the car, sell it at auction, and the proceeds would go to you. Now you're saying you'd give me the proceeds? That could be a lot of money. Why would you do that?"

She gazed off in the distance. How could she tell him that she didn't need the money without sounding like a spoiled untouchable heiress? More importantly, how could she tell him he was the most exciting thing to ever happen to her? It was like waking up with some to-die-for celebrity eager to take you in their arms and kiss—

Nico waved a hand in front of her face. "Lily?"

She turned back to him. "Yup."

"Why?"

"Just think about it," she said. "A week out there, a week back, stopping to see the sights along the way by day…" She stared at the toe of his work boot and blurted, "Staying at nice hotels at night." She hoped she'd gotten her message across. This was brand-new territory for her. Propositioning a gorgeous man.

"Your dad would kill me."

Her head snapped up to see he'd clearly read between the lines.

"I mean *destroy* me," he said. "He's my best client."

"My dad would never know. I swear."

He studied her for a moment, his gaze drifting to her mouth before snapping back to her eyes. "Let me see if I understand this correctly. We would share a hotel room?"

"Correct." She really liked his sharp mind. "For two weeks." That should be enough time for her to become a very experienced, very satisfied woman. She'd move to the city for her new job as a confident twenty-something single ready to mingle. A new Lily. A new life.

"Why would you offer me all this?" he asked. "A car? You, if I get your meaning."

She bit her lip. She could never tell him she'd only been with one man. He'd think she was pathetic. She went with something that would make them both feel good. "You are smoking hot."

He grinned. "You tempt me, but…" He slowly shook his head like he was going to turn her down.

She made one last-ditch effort, lowering her voice to a seductive slutty vixen purr. "Two weeks, Nico. Then you go here, I go there. The end." It was both a no-strings offer and a practical statement. She knew better than to get her hopes up that he'd want anything long term. He was the kind of man who could get any woman. He'd likely marry one day years in the future to a woman of equal movie-star hotness.

He stepped closer. "Where's there?"

"New York City. I got a job at the Earth Defense Group." She made a fist. "Fighting the good fight on behalf of the earth."

Nico stepped back and resumed pacing. She pulled an old receipt from her purse, scribbled down her number on the back, and held it out to him. "Call me once you've had a chance to think it over."

He stopped pacing, took the number, and stuffed it in his jeans pocket. "How much you want for the Mustang?"

"I told you I'd give it to you."

"What's your dad going to think about you giving me the car?"

"He'll never know. Just restore it and put it up for auction as planned. Only difference is you pocket the money instead of sending me a check."

He looked like he was thinking hard.

"It's my car," she said. "I can do what I want with it."

He nodded once. "I'm in."

Her stomach dropped. Omigod, it was really happening. She gripped her hands tightly together to hide the fact that they were shaking. *Come on, Lily, you can do this.*

Nico went on. "We'll figure a good price once I see

it."

She shook her head. No money would pass between them for this sex tutorial, err, road trip. "I told you, I don't need the money. I've got a trust fund. And, by the way, just in case that gets you excited, I'll give my standard lawyer-like disclaimer: prenup mandatory."

He gave her a strange look. "You always tell guys you just met they have to sign a prenup?"

"Pretty much."

He cocked his head, considering her. "How's that working out for ya?"

She lifted her chin. "Just fine."

He shook his head, a small smile playing around his lips. Okay, maybe it was a little strange, and it certainly hadn't worked in her favor, but at least she didn't have the heartbreak down the line of finding out the whole thing was a sham.

"No worries," Nico said with a big smile and a wink. "Marriage is definitely not on the agenda for me."

That was as she'd expected. He'd never want someone like her when he could—oh! He'd kissed her cheek, which instantly yanked her from her painful thoughts. She felt all lit up inside when he kissed her, even on the cheek.

He tucked a lock of hair behind her ear. "I've never been propositioned with a car before."

Her cheeks burned, and her hands fluttered in the

air. "It wasn't a proposition." And the car was so beside the point.

His mouth curled in a slow, sexy smile that made her knees go weak. "Yeah, it was. And I'm extremely flattered."

She was speechless. Completely frozen in place and speechless.

His voice rumbled in her ear. "That was hot."

Still speechless.

His voice kept rumbling in her ear, sending shivers through her. "I only hesitated because of your dad, but what he doesn't know won't hurt him. Right?"

She nodded, hoping she'd regain the power of speech soon.

He ran a hand from her shoulder down her arm, leaving a hot tingle in his wake before squeezing her hand. "I'll see you next Saturday."

She nodded again, almost dizzy with the idea of two weeks in this man's bed. It was an embarrassment of riches to be with the incredibly gorgeous, sexy, kiss-stealing Nico after her dry spell. Still, she should get to know him a little better before they got naked. Right?

She cleared her throat. "What's your last name?"

He barked out a laugh. "Marino. See you soon, Lily Spencer." He headed back into the garage.

She swallowed hard and summoned her inner slutty vixen. "Can't wait!"

CHAPTER FOUR

Nico sat at the crowded oak dining room table in his parents' ranch-style home for their regular Sunday night family dinner and announced, "I'm going to miss the next couple of Sunday dinners, but I'll be back in time for Vince's wedding."

Vince, his older brother by two years, immediately got to the most important point. "What about my bachelor party?"

Vince's dark brows shot up in question over dark brown eyes. They resembled each other—same dark hair, dark eyes, and olive skin, except Vince was a bulky, hulking man, taller and broader. He used to be a star football player, now in construction. Nico had gotten lucky in the gene pool, a combination of his parents' looks that made him, the middle son, a happy medium between hulking man (Vince) and shrimpy sweet-faced man (his younger brother, Angel).

"Maybe," Nico said. He didn't want to cut the trip

short. He only had Lily in his bed for two weeks. He figured a week there, a week back. More like thirteen days with the rehearsal dinner that he really needed to be at the night before the wedding. He was one of five best men. Vince had asked all of his brothers, two biological (the Marinos), three step (the Reynolds), to act as best men. The Marinos were all dark-haired, dark-eyed Italians, the Reynolds all fair-skinned, light brown to dirty blond hair, and blue eyes. Except Jared, who got green eyes from some Reynolds ancestor.

"Maybe?" Vince boomed. "That's the most important part. My last night of freedom!"

"Oh, really?" his fiancée, Sophia, asked from where she sat at his side. She had long brown hair, deep brown eyes, and a gorgeous body, though Nico tried not to notice. She was an Italian beauty with a fiery temper. "That's the most important part? What am I—"

Her reply was cut off as Vince wrapped an arm around her, hauled her close, and kissed her a little longer than was appropriate in front of their dad, stepmom, five brothers, sister-in-law, and baby nephew.

Vince finally let her up for air. "Sorry, sweetheart, you're the most important part. You know that. I was just joking. I love you."

Sophia was staring at his mouth. "Hmph."

Looking pleased with her response, Vince lifted his arm off her shoulders and went back to eating the delicious manicotti. The two of them always cracked Nico up. Sophia kept Vince in line, but Vince sort of handled her too.

"Where are you heading?" his petite blond stepmother asked. His mom had died when he was only seven, and he'd been lucky to get Allie as a stepmother a few years later. She'd taken in him and his brothers, Vince and Angel, as her own. She'd even written a picture book series featuring her sons, Gabe, Luke, and Jared as hedgehogs, and him and his brothers as porcupines. She cemented a place deep in his heart when he'd seen that. They were family from that point on.

"I'm taking a road trip to California," Nico said.

"You deserve a vacation," his stepmom said. "I can't remember the last time you took one."

He sliced off a piece of manicotti. "Yeah, well, if I don't work, I don't make money. I still need a hundred grand more to buy out Kevin."

"Are you going alone?" Angel asked with some concern. His youngest brother was a couple inches shorter than him, all lean muscle. His always-rumpled dark brown hair and dimpled smile gave him the angelic look of a priest. He practically was one, devoted to one woman for years that he never touched.

He'd become a social worker and was always looking out for their emotional well-being.

Nico smiled to himself, thinking of the sexy Lily. "I'll have company."

"I saw that horndog smile," Luke said, his dark blue eyes crinkling with a horndog smile of his own. His stepbrother was sporting a neatly trimmed beard to go with his two-hundred-dollar haircut. Were those blond highlights in his hair? His usual dirty blond hair looked lighter. Damn, he was turning total city hipster. As if the expensive tailored suits weren't enough. "Who's the woman?"

"Nico has a girlfriend?" his sister-in-law, Zoe, asked, her brown eyes lighting up. Ever since she'd married Gabe, she'd been hoping all of Gabe's brothers would find the kind of lasting love that they had. A nice sentiment, but not all of them were meant for that. Nico had been married once. Ava had left him, pregnant with another man's child. He'd made her get a paternity test to be sure. Never again would he let a woman in close enough to rip his heart to shreds. Marriage was out of the question.

"Really?" Gabe asked, sounding doubtful.

Nico speared some manicotti. "Not a girlfriend. Just someone I met."

"Is it the redhead?" Luke asked.

"Ooh," Jared chimed in, "I dig redheads." His

younger stepbrother was an orthopedic surgeon and busy working his way through the pretty nurses at the hospital. It was a practical way to meet women since Jared was nearly always working. Where else would he meet someone?

Nico stuffed manicotti in his mouth, done talking about it. He nodded once at Luke, hoping he'd drop it.

"The one who slapped you?" Luke asked.

Nico scowled as all of his brothers laughed. Even his dad. The women looked at him with concern. Stupid Luke already knew both redheads had slapped him.

He discreetly scratched his cheek with his middle finger as he looked at Luke across the table, knowing his stepmom would object to the full-on gesture. She demanded nice manners at family dinners.

Luke grinned mischievously. "Sounds feisty."

Vince piped up. "The feisty ones are good in the— OW!" He turned to Sophia, who must've got him good under the table. At the loud exclamation from Vince, his five-month-old nephew, Miles, startled and burst into tears.

"Now you made my godson cry," Vince said to Sophia. He stood and walked around the table to Miles' highchair near his parents Gabe and Zoe. "C'mere, little man. Time for a motorcycle ride."

He lifted the baby out, settled him on his stomach across his forearm, and did a slow turn around the dining room. Miles immediately quieted down, his wispy dark hair sticking up a little as he looked around on his tour.

Luke gestured for Vince to continue. "Good in the what?"

Vince jerked his chin at Luke. "Instigator."

Zoe smiled at Sophia. "I bet you can't wait to have his babies."

"He has his moments," Sophia replied with a smile.

His stepmom looked right at Nico, love in her eyes. "We'll certainly miss you around here, but I hope this trip is just what you need."

"Thanks, Ma." He hadn't missed a Sunday family dinner in years. He had a routine: work, weekend hookups, and Sunday dinner. So what if he felt a little lonely sometimes, kicking around his cheap studio apartment. He'd taken it to save money. Everything he did was toward one goal—becoming full owner of his shop. His stepmom was right. This road trip was just what he needed, both a vacation with a beautiful woman and a chance at the barn find that could bring the big bucks.

"Hey, Nic, I'll be in Chicago next Sunday," Luke said. "If you think you'll be there by then, we could meet up for dinner."

Nico considered. He'd already confirmed with Lily by text that they'd be leaving early Saturday morning. They could probably reach Cleveland by Saturday night, Chicago by Sunday dinner.

"Sure," Nico said. "But if you hit on Lily, you're dead."

"Ooh, Lily, she has a name!" Jared pronounced.

His stepmom gave his dad a significant look. Nico felt his ears burn. He never mentioned any of his casual hookups by name.

"Maybe when you come back, you could bring Lily by for dinner," his stepmom said. Nico hadn't brought a woman home since his ex-wife. He had no intention of starting now.

"Yeah," Vince chimed in with a wide smile. His brother was just loving the fact that his stepmom was focused on him now for her matchmaking. She'd already pulled that on Vince, offering Sophia Italian wedding soup and Italian wedding cookies the first time he'd brought her home. "Make the cookies, Ma," Vince added.

"Don't make the cookies," Nico said. "I'm not bringing her for dinner."

"Nico's in love," Luke teased. If he'd been within reach, Nico would've socked him.

"Shut up," Nico snapped instead.

His stepmom took pity on him and steered the conversation to the much safer topic of Vince and Sophia's wedding and rehearsal dinner. Vince settled at the table with Miles, who was already drifting off, leaning against Vince's chest.

"I think all the best men should give a toast to Vince and Sophia," his dad said. Ever since his cancer scare—he'd been given a clean bill of health after surgery and follow-up chemo for colon cancer—his dad had been a lot more sentimental.

"I think that's nice," his stepmom said.

"Me too," Sophia said.

Vince sat there, quiet for once, the tips of his ears red.

"My speech will be all about how you tamed him, Soph," Nico said to the laughter of his brothers. Except Vince, who gazed at Sophia with total adoration. "And saved us all!"

"Hear, hear," Luke said.

They all toasted to that.

Vince just shook his head. "I'm damn lucky."

"Aww!" Zoe exclaimed. "Look how happy he is, Nico. You're next, I swear!"

He held up his palms. "I'm doing just fine."

Luke grinned. "I'll report back to you all after I meet her."

Nico groaned.

"Please do," his stepmom said. Everyone agreed just to tease him.

He shook his head and continued eating. He and Lily had worked it out already. Two weeks, no strings. And while he could hold his own in the wealthy circles of the elite that made up his clients and the big spenders he met at the parties Luke invited him to in the city, he didn't kid himself for one moment that he had anything to offer someone like that other than a good time. He was a grease monkey, no more, no less, and that was just fine with him. His stepmom would just have to be disappointed.

But he'd enjoy every minute with Lily. He already knew from that kiss they'd be good together. It was exactly the kind of easy, fun time he lived for. A brief stab of worry about her dad and the wrath he could rain down on him clouded his good-time vision, but he pushed that away. She swore she wouldn't tell him, and he certainly wasn't going to mention it. What could go wrong?

~ ~ ~

Nico drove into work the next morning beyond excited about the car Lily had described. He'd done his research last night on 1969 Ford Mustangs. The value could go from the low five figures up to half a million, depending on the type of car. The low end was hardly worth his time, but the chance of being the first to get his hands on the high end, on the ultimate untouched barn find, the Boss 429, was enough to make him want to dance. And he wasn't a dancing kind of guy. It wasn't just the money, though he desperately wanted to buy out Kevin, it was the ultimate for a car lover like him to get his hands on a treasure like that. He'd have to sell it, but he'd enjoy it a bit first, show it off in a few car shows.

It was all within reach. He'd finally be a success.

And then there was Lily, the sweet cherry on top. Two weeks of open road by day, two weeks of tearing up the sheets at night. Hell yeah. And it was all so clear cut and neat. She'd go on to her place in the city, no hard feelings. But he would enjoy those two weeks immensely. Nico had kissed plenty of women, but it had been a helluva long time since he'd actually lost himself in the moment. He was all smooth technique, a well-choreographed routine to get from point A to point B efficiently. Lily had made him greedy, hungry, and want with a fierceness that shook him up.

He eyed the flatbed truck at the far end of the parking lot as he pulled in. He planned on taking the truck to retrieve the Mustang. It suddenly occurred to him that Lily might not know how to drive a truck, let alone a stick shift, and while he could do all the driving, he always thought it was safer to take driving in shifts so no one got too tired at the wheel.

He smiled to himself. Who was he kidding? He just wanted to see her again. He parked his Porsche and called her.

"Yes?" she answered, still sounding half asleep. It was eight a.m.

"Hey, it's Nico."

"Oh!"

"What're you doing today?"

"Sleeping. What time is it?"

"Eight."

"Oh."

Silence. Had she gone back to sleep? He imagined that red hair tousled, her electric blue eyes slowly shutting, that mouth with the cute bow and plump lower lip. He adjusted himself. He was getting turned on just thinking about her mouth. "Lily?"

"Hmm?"

"Are you awake?"

"Barely."

"Stop by the shop once you wake up. I want to teach you to drive the truck. It's a stick shift. Noon okay?"

"What truck?"

"I need to take the flatbed truck to haul the Mustang back."

"M'kay. Bye."

She didn't hang up. He could hear her breathing. He shook his head with a smile and disconnected. He should probably call back later in case she had no memory of their conversation.

~ ~ ~

Lily showed up at Nico's shop at noon all dolled up. She had to distract him from her complete lack of coordination. She just knew driving a stick shift was going to be impossible. Her dad had tried to teach her once on his Mercedes. He ended up yelling at her, she ended up in tears, and that was the end of driving a stick shift. It was just so hard to remember which pedal to press when—there were three pedals and she only had two feet—at the same time as she was supposed to be moving the shifter thing. She wore shorts that showed plenty of leg and a loose V-neck white T-shirt that didn't cling to her middle. Contacts, of course. She hoped to avoid her glasses entirely on their trip, though he might see her in them in the early morning before she had a chance to put the contacts in. Not that there was anything wrong with glasses, but when she wore them at law school, she'd been mistaken for a professor more than once. They made her look smart, older, and way too dignified to have a casual fling with.

She stopped at the garage first, suddenly very eager

to see him. He'd called her a second time an hour ago, which made her think he really, really wanted to see her. She peeked in at the men working on cars in there. No Nico. She headed into the showroom. Still no sign of him.

She eyed the door of his office, went hot all over thinking of the last time she'd been in there, took a deep breath and headed on over. She knocked and waited.

"Hello," a deep voice said from very close behind her.

She whirled. "Hi!"

Nico smiled, and she melted. That smile was killer—part wicked, part charming, and oh so sexy. "Did you eat?"

"Eat what?" she breathed.

He took her by the elbow and walked with her through the showroom. Her elbow tingled. "Did you eat lunch?"

She'd been too nervous to eat. "Yes."

"I didn't. Do you mind if we just grab something real quick?"

"No. Yes."

He stopped and looked at her, his brows coming together. "Which is it?"

"I don't mind."

"There's a good pizza place a short drive from

here."

She nodded. He led her to a gorgeous shiny red Porsche. He probably washed and waxed it daily. He opened the door for her and guided her in. She sank into the leather seat.

Nico got in, and she discreetly breathed him in, the sharp lingering scent of oil, some kind of musky cologne, and warm Italian stud. She couldn't believe she'd get to be with him for two whole weeks. He grabbed the stick shift, put it into gear, and peeled out of the lot.

"So you ever drive a stick shift?" he asked.

"Once, but it was so long ago I completely forget how. I hope you're a patient teacher."

"Sure, I've taught lots of people. It's nothing."

"I'm in your hands."

He glanced over at her and gave her a sexy smile that made her stomach do a delicious flip. "The truck has a different feel for it than a stick-shift car, a few more gears, so it's good you're starting practically new on it."

"Truck virgin here!" she exclaimed way too loudly.

He chuckled. He really was good-looking, almost too good-looking. Her stomach went from warm melt to a slow churn. Nerves settled in. "I mean, not literally."

He tilted his head toward her. "Not literally

what?"

"Not literally a virgin," she choked out. Why had she said that?

"Oh-kay."

"I mean, I *am* a truck virgin, but not, you know, the other kind." Shut up. Just shut up.

He laughed, so she laughed too. Only hers came out high-pitched like a nervous, maniacal, twenty-five-year-old virgin. Which she wasn't. She'd done it bunches of times with lots of lovers.

In her imagination.

She should probably tell him she'd only been with one man who had to close his eyes and think of someone else to sleep with her. *No, don't tell him that! He'll never sleep with you.*

"I'm not totally the other way either," she blurted.

"What other way?"

She should really try not to talk when she was nervous. She'd been about to say she wasn't totally slutty, but that wasn't going to help her case either. "Never mind."

He reached over and squeezed her hand. "I'll take you any way I can get."

He gave her a panty-melting smile that really, really worked. Maybe there was hope for her yet.

CHAPTER FIVE

There was seriously no hope for her. She spilled pizza sauce on the front of her shirt after she'd tried so hard to eat her slice with delicate care. Then she'd tried to clean it off at the sink in the ladies' room, which was thankfully a small private bathroom, and somehow managed to soak the front and spread the stain mostly over one breast. She felt like crying. Now she had to get through a stick-shift lesson, which she knew she'd screw up, wearing a very unsexy stained T-shirt. She turned on the hand dryer and lifted her shirt under it. The sauce was more orange than red now.

She was so far out of her league.

Maybe she could sneak out the back. It was such a small restaurant, though, he might see her in the hallway. There was a small window above the bathroom stall. If she stood on the toilet and she could somehow hoist herself up. But could she fit? What if she got stuck?

Someone knocked on the ladies' room door. She'd been in here for a really long time.

"Lily?" Nico called. "You okay?"

She cleared her throat. "Yes."

"Okay."

She eyed the window again. She couldn't chance getting stuck. She'd look like Pooh bear stuck in his hole from eating too much honey. She took the shirt off and looked at it. Backwards? Inside out? Which was better? She tore the tag off and put it on inside out. There. She fussed with her hair and reapplied her favorite cherry, tinted lip balm before taking a deep breath and unlocking the bathroom door.

She turned to go back to their table and nearly ran into Nico standing in the hallway. His gaze dropped to her chest. "What happened to your shirt?"

"A little spill. But I fixed it."

He leaned down to her ear. "I can see right through it."

She glanced down to see that the shirt, once inside out, had soaked right through her bra and her nipples were like headlights pointing right at him. She crossed her arms over herself. "I'm such a klutz," she whispered.

And then he was unbuttoning his work shirt.

"What are you doing?" she asked, slightly alarmed at the idea of a bare-chested Nico. She might spontaneously combust.

He kept unbuttoning, and she realized, thankfully, that he wore a white undershirt.

"Hold this," he said, handing her the navy blue shirt embroidered with his name. He pulled his undershirt over his head in one quick two-handed move and handed it to her. Her jaw dropped. He had muscles, like, everywhere—shoulders, biceps, pecs, tight six-pack abs. Her hand came up of its own accord to touch all that beautiful olive skin, but he snagged his work shirt out of her other hand and was already covering up. He jerked his chin at her. "Go change and meet me out front."

She nodded like a bobble-head and returned to the ladies' room. She took off the stained T-shirt and tossed it in the garbage. A quick boob dry under the dryer, and she slipped his undershirt over her head. It was still warm from his body. His scent of oil, deodorant, and Nico surrounded her; she felt almost woozy from it. It was too long, of course, the shoulders drooped down too low. The end hit the top of her legs. She debated tucking it in or leaving it loose.

She looked in the mirror and tucked it in. Nope. Too much fabric giving her a tire-around-the-middle look. Nightgown it was. She sighed. So much for distracting him with her sexy outfit during what she was sure would be a disastrous driving lesson.

~ ~ ~

Nico rubbed the back of his neck, working on getting the image of Lily's hard nipples pointing at him out of his head. He couldn't teach her to drive stick if he was spending all his time figuring the fastest way to get her flat on her back. She finally stepped out of the restaurant, wearing those large, round shades and a pout that made her lips look even more sinfully delicious. His undershirt fit her like a sexy nightie, and he broke out in a sweat, thinking of the nights ahead where he'd get to see her in one and then out of one.

"Thanks for the shirt," she said softly.

"Don't worry about it." His voice came out harsh on account of all his wayward thoughts fighting to get out. He wanted to proposition her. He wanted to start their casual affair right now. His office would work.

She trailed behind him, still pouty. It occurred to him that maybe she was upset she'd ruined her shirt. He crossed back to her, grabbed her hand, and walked with her to his car. "Hey, don't worry about that shirt. Mine looks great on you. Even better than that other one."

"Yeah?" she asked. "Are you teasing?"

"Yeah."

She frowned.

"I mean, no, I'm not teasing. Yeah, it does look good."

They got to his car, and he opened the door for her. She pushed her shades up to the top of her head and met his eyes, those electric blues jolting him again. "It's much too big. It looks like a nightgown."

He couldn't help himself. He traced the bow in her upper lip with his finger, and then slowly traced to her lower lip. Her lips parted as he pressed on the plump softness of her lower lip. He was obsessed with her mouth. He dropped his hand and stole a quick kiss that sent a rush of heat through his system. He pulled back before he got in too deep. "I keep imagining that T-shirt is all you have on."

"O-oh," she said, her face flushing pink. She put her hands to her cheeks.

Her response puzzled him. He studied her for a moment. She seemed almost virginal.

He turned and headed for the other side of the car, sliding into the driver's seat. She got in and put on her seatbelt. She looked ridiculously sexy wearing his oversized shirt, the hem sliding along her upper thigh haphazardly. It really did look like she had nothing on underneath.

He pulled out of the lot. "If you don't mind me asking, how old are you?"

"Twenty-five. Why?"

He shook his head. No way she was a virgin at twenty-five. And not the way she'd kissed him the other day. "Just curious."

She slid her shades back on. "How old are you?"

"Thirty-two."

"Then we're all legal."

One corner of his mouth lifted. He'd almost forgotten she was a lawyer. His stepbrother Gabe was a lawyer too, helluva good guy. He had no problem with the lawyer part. The waiting part was the difficult thing. Geez, he really was a horndog. He could wait until the weekend. Six days wouldn't kill him.

~ ~ ~

Lily was killing him. It wasn't that she kept hitting the gas instead of the brake, or that she kept grinding the gears, or even that she'd nearly gotten them killed full speed in reverse. It was the way she kept biting her bottom lip. The way she squeaked and squealed as she drove terribly, excitable and noisy. The way she turned to him with a laughing apology, her smile lighting up her face as she begged him for one more try. She was entirely too appealing for someone he had to wait six days to see naked.

"Stop!" he hollered after twenty minutes of a roller coaster between pure terror and raw lust.

She accelerated accidentally before slamming on the brakes, and his seatbelt jerked as he flew forward. Luckily they were in a large empty parking lot, so she was only putting him in danger.

"What? I'm terrible, aren't I?" She shook a finger at him. "I warned you."

He pinched the bridge of his nose and shut his eyes. "We'll try again tomorrow."

"We will?" She sounded hopeful and a little excited.

He looked at her. She beamed, her bright blue eyes shining, cheeks pink and round. There was a light sprinkle of freckles across her cute, upturned nose that he hadn't noticed before. His heart did a weird kerthunk.

"You just need practice," he said gruffly.

Her hand fluttered in the air. "Oh! I thought for sure you'd be mad." She threw her arms around his neck and hugged him. She smelled so sweet and fresh with a hint of cherries. She pulled back. "Thank you for being so patient. I'll try to remember what you said, clutch then gas. First gear is very important."

He pressed his lips together, trying not to laugh. A few other gears were important too, but whatever. "Not bad for a first lesson. Lunch and lesson tomorrow?"

She nodded happily.

"Let's switch places." He got out of the truck, the feel of the solid ground under his feet a relief after that ride. She strode by him in that nightie, hips swaying, and he turned to see the rear view. Peekaboo with the edge of her shorts nearly did him in. He turned back and got in the truck.

"You're a great teacher, Nico," she said.

She was a terrible student, but so enthusiastic he couldn't say anything about it. "Thanks."

~ ~ ~

Lily sat across from Nico the next day at a deli, pretending to eat and distracting him from her non-eating by talking up a storm. There was no way on this second meeting he was going to see her spill food all over herself. Instead she was sharing, perhaps oversharing, about law school. He was a really good listener, so she launched into the story about her stuffy first year law-school professor, who she'd tried to make laugh by holding up a series of signs.

"So I figured he was so stiff because he was nervous, you know?" she asked. "I mean, he always stared at a point on the back wall like he was pretending the fifty of us weren't there."

"Aren't you going to eat your sub?" Nico asked.

"Yes." She stole one of his potato chips because it seemed less messy. "Anyway, after a week of this completely robotic lecture, I held up a sign that said 'my expectations are set reassuringly low.'"

Nico snorted. "Did you get kicked out of class?"

"No, he laughed. Of course, that just encouraged me, so the next day I held up a sign that said, 'Pretend we're not here.'"

Nico shook his head. "What school was this?"

"Yale. My family are alums."

"What's that mean?" He unscrewed the cap on a bottled water and took a long swallow.

"That means many Spencers have graduated from there, and they like to keep letting Spencers in. Anyway, long story short, I nailed him."

Nico spewed his water. She cracked up.

He coughed a bunch and wiped his eyes. "You did not."

She grinned. "No. But he did thank me for it. Said it was his first time teaching, and he looked forward to my signs."

"Did you do a different one every day?" Nico asked.

"Yup. For about a month. Then he relaxed, so I dropped it."

"You're something. Eat your lunch."

"I'm not hungry."

"Did you eat already?"

"No."

"I'm not getting in that truck with a hungry woman. You might be on edge and then—" he whistled and gestured with one fist hitting his palm

"—*crash*."

She stared at the sub with ham, cheese, shredded lettuce, sliced tomatoes, and some oil and vinegar that would surely end up all over her shirt.

"I'll let you wear my shirt if you spill," he said. He was a pretty sharp guy. She liked that. On the other hand, he must think she was a total klutz, which was super embarrassing and not sexy. Then again, if she did spill, she'd get another peek at a shirtless Nico.

"You looked cute in my shirt," he added with a wink. "So I hope you do spill."

She couldn't help but smile. She took a bite and a tomato fell out the other side. Luckily, it hit the table and not her shirt.

He leaned back, already finished his sub. "I'll wait. Go ahead and finish."

"Not in a hurry to get back in that truck with me, are you?"

"I'm sure you'll get the hang of things today."

She grinned. "I'm sure I will too." She took another bite of sub and chewed. "Tell me about you. You always want to be a mechanic?"

"I wanted to be a firefighter that rode a dinosaur, but then I grew up."

She laughed. He grinned, his chocolate brown eyes dancing with amusement. "Yeah, I've always liked cars. I started working at the shop when I was sixteen. I was lucky to work with Kevin, my old boss, he's an expert on Ferraris and knows a helluva lot about all the classic cars. I love it."

She listened and chewed as he told her all about classic cars and the intricacies involved in the restoration of them.

He stopped himself. "You didn't need to hear all that."

"I liked it. I think it's wonderful that you love what you do. Not everyone has a job they love."

He inclined his head. "The best part is now I'm the boss."

"So you own the shop?" she asked before taking another bite of sub.

He bristled and crumpled up the wrapper from his sub. "Almost. I will soon. I'm working on buying out Kevin's stake. He's still part owner."

She chewed and swallowed. "Guess my barn find could help with that."

"Exactly. That's why I can't wait to go."

Her hopes dashed. Here she'd thought they were getting along so well. Maybe even flirting a little. He'd kissed her twice, which had been amazing, at least for her. It was probably nothing to him.

She nodded. "Of course." She swallowed hard. "I hope it's worth it for you. I don't even know what kind of car it is."

He crossed his arms. "I'll take my chances."

She set her sub down, appetite gone. She felt foolish for all the time she spent fantasizing about Nico actually wanting her. Of course he just wanted the car and the money it would bring him. Everything came down to money.

"You done?" he asked.

She nodded and carefully tucked the wrapper around the half sandwich remaining. "Yup. I'm ready for lesson number two." She forced a smile. "This'll be fun. I think I'm getting the hang of it."

"Great," he said. "I look forward to kissing the dashboard again." He winked, and her hopes rose once again. Augh. She was being naive. Just because a gorgeous man was great at flirting didn't mean it was anything personal. He was probably flirty and winky with every woman he met.

She stood and tossed the rest of her lunch in the trash. "You won't kiss the dashboard this time. Promise."

He leaned close, his voice a husky drawl. "I'm holding you to that promise."

Her breath caught. He took her hand and walked her out the door. He was always touching her. How was she not supposed to get the wrong idea? Maybe that's just how he was, touching women all the time. She just wasn't used to it. She'd grown up in a rather formal household, and she'd only had the one boyfriend. John had only touched her in bed.

When they got to the empty parking lot behind the warehouse once more, Nico stopped the truck and looked at her from the driver's seat. "Ready?"

"Ready," she answered with a smile.

"Go!"

They got out and ran around the front of the truck to switch places. She giggled as she passed him smiling at her. She hopped in, waited for them both to put their seatbelts on, and tried to remember his instructions.

First step, start the truck. It made a huge, weird noise.

"It's on!" Nico cried. "Didn't you hear the engine?"

"I'm sorry! I was just trying to remember everything. Okay, I got it. So, first gear."

After a few misstarts and a wrong gear, she was feeling pretty good about the way she went from first to second and didn't go in reverse at all. After about half an hour of wonderfully smooth lessons with only a few stalls and sudden braking incidents, Nico stopped her.

"I think that's good," he said. "I'll take it from here."

"You sure? Maybe I should practice a little more."

"Tomorrow," he said firmly. She worried for a minute that she'd screwed up and that he was mad, but then he chucked her under the chin and smiled. "Okay?"

"Okay." She would've agreed to anything with that killer smile. And the casual way he kept touching her. This would be a piece of cake to get him to sleep with her. Of course, once they were in bed, he'd realize she had no clue. Augh. Nerves gripped her. Maybe this whole sleeping together thing was a bad idea. She didn't want him to laugh at her, or worse, pretend she was someone hotter, or, God forbid, stare at her poundage. What in the world was she doing with the gorgeous Nico? He only wanted her for her car. She was fooling herself.

He got out of the truck and walked around to switch places again, so she did the same. When she passed him in front of the truck, he gave her an enthusiastic high five, making her spirits lift. Maybe the lessons weren't going as badly as she'd thought. Maybe the gorgeous Nico wouldn't mind teaching her a thing or two more. In bed.

CHAPTER SIX

Nico finally had to cry uncle after a hair-raising turn that nearly tipped the truck sideways. It had been five days, and they still hadn't left the empty parking lot.

"Brake!" he hollered.

Lily slammed on the brakes, jerking them both against their seatbelts, and then the truck stalled out.

"I know what to do," Lily said, hitting the clutch and starting the truck again.

"Ya know what?" Nico asked.

She turned, her expression open and eager. "What?"

"I could do the driving on this trip."

"You sure? It's a lot of miles, and I really think I'm improving."

Seriously? "How's that now?"

She smiled serenely. "I always remember the emergency brake once the truck is off. No more rolling."

He nodded. "That's good."

"Yes, and I'm stalling less."

"True…" He really didn't want to hurt her feelings. She'd been a trooper coming back day after day for terrible driving lessons. She *tried*. She really did. "I like driving, though. I don't mind."

She blew out a breath. "Oh, good. I didn't want to say anything, but it would really help me out if you did. Then I could study for the bar exam."

He'd nearly gotten killed all week, scared a few years off his life, and struggled with his unaccountable lust under extreme conditions, and she didn't even *want* to drive?

He shook his head slowly. "So, all this time, you were being…nice?"

"Well, you seemed so set on teaching me. I figured it was the least I could do. I mean, I did ask you to take me on this road trip. I didn't want you to have to do all the work."

He leaned his head back on the seat and let out an exasperated breath. He jolted upright as the truck started rolling. "Brake!"

She slammed on the brake, and they halted abruptly. "Oops."

"Turn off the truck," he said through his teeth.

She turned the key, remembered the emergency brake, and everything went quiet as the truck shut off.

He took a deep breath. It was fine. No one had gotten killed. So what if he'd suffered? It would all be worth it. He'd get the barn find he wanted, maybe even the holy grail of cars, and by tomorrow night he'd finally get to have Lily. He purposely hadn't kissed her again because he'd have her under him in two seconds flat and that was no way to teach someone to drive. He forced his mind away from that thought and focused instead on the irritating fact that he'd tortured himself for no good reason. He'd had the worst case of blue balls all week.

She pushed her shades to the top of her head and met his eyes. "This would've been easier if we took my Prius."

"I'm six foot two. You think I can fit in that tin can? And how the hell could I tow a car with it? It'd probably burn out the engine."

She pursed her sexy-as-sin lips. "You are mad. I tried really hard, you know."

He couldn't take it anymore. He wrapped his hand around the back of her neck and pulled her close, settling his mouth against hers, taking the hungry kiss he'd been dying for all week. He tasted her and lost himself. There was nothing but her soft mouth and an urgent driving need for more. He desperately wished there wasn't a console between them as he needed more of him pressed against more of her. She made this little mewling noise in the back of her throat that made him crazy. He kissed her, devoured her, and found himself leaning across the truck, trying to press closer. He tore his mouth from hers. "Let's go back to my office for a quickie."

She shifted away from him.

"What's wrong?" he asked.

She stared straight ahead. "I'm not like you, Nico, okay? I can't just whip it out in the middle of the day in an office and then go about my business."

His lips twitched. What in the world would she whip out? "I'm sorry. I got…I don't know. I got really into it. I've been thinking about you all week."

She looked at him under her lashes, almost shyly. "You have?"

He took her hand and held it. "Yeah. You said I'd get two weeks of sleeping with you. No strings. Remember?"

She flushed and mumbled something.

He tipped her chin up. "What're you mumbling there?"

She looked at a point over his shoulder. "I said two weeks starts on Saturday."

"That's tomorrow."

"Yup."

"Lily?"

"What?"

He waited until she met his eyes again and read uncertainty there. "You want out of our deal?" *Please say no.* Hooking up with the sexy Lily was half the reason he wanted to go on this trip so badly. Fast becoming the main reason he wanted to go.

She looked him up and down, licking her lips, which sent a jolt to his groin. "No."

He let out a breath of relief. "Okay, then." He rubbed the back of his neck. "So I guess you want someplace nicer than my back office."

She nodded. "And not a quickie. A slowie."

He laughed, and she stiffened. Shit. He hadn't meant to laugh at her. It just sounded funny. A slowie.

He slid his hand into her soft red hair, stroked his thumb over her cheek, and whispered in her ear, "It'll be so slow you'll be begging for fast."

She sucked in an audible breath.

He pulled back to look in her blue eyes. "Promise."

"O-o-oh," she sighed.

He loved her responses, so open and honest. He pressed a thumb to her lower lip and into her hot mouth. She sucked it, and his cock pulsed. He stifled a groan. He spent entirely too much time thinking about that mouth, those pink full lips with the bow at the top. He dropped his hand. "Switch places."

They got out, switched, and he pulled out of the

lot.

"Thank you," she said softly. "For understanding."

"No problem." It was a problem. It would be hell to take things slow, but he'd do it. At least the first night to put her at ease.

"I've got our route all planned out," she said, "taking route eighty west clear across the country with stops at a few scenic places, and, if we have lunch on the road, we can still stop for nice dinners and relaxing evenings."

"Relaxing, huh? I guess eventually we'll be relaxed." He glanced over to find her blushing. He had that uneasy feeling again that she was inexperienced, but he didn't want to come out and ask her if she was a virgin. That would be insulting. Still, he had to know what he was working with here.

"You, uh," he started. Sleep with a lot of guys? Sleep with any guys? He didn't know how to ask. He'd never had this strange experience before. The women he hooked up with were all very well experienced.

"What?"

"You ever…" Why was this so hard? "What kind of guys you usually date?" There. Nice and neutral.

She shrugged. "Does it matter?"

"No." He tried again. "What're you into?" He congratulated himself on the subtlety of the question that would surely give him the answer he needed to know.

"I love crochet, and I'm a real sucker for superhero movies. Don't even get me started on Norse mythology!"

He nodded. "Cool."

"What're you into?" she asked, all innocence.

She was going to be the death of him.

CHAPTER SEVEN

Lily showed up at Nico's shop on time early Saturday morning with a large suitcase in tow. She'd worn a purple wrap dress with a deep V that showed off her cleavage, and had spent two hours trying to get her hair to fall in careless waves and also apply makeup that looked like it wasn't there. She knew she was trying too hard. Who traveled all dressed up in a truck? But she figured it was her only chance of impressing Nico on this trip. After a while, her clothes would all be wrinkled, and she'd be too busy traveling to fuss for long with her appearance.

"Hey, *bella*," he said, greeting her with a warm honey voice and that killer smile.

Her stomach did a few flips. "Hey, *bello*." She cocked her head. "Is that right?"

"Sure is. Nice dress."

She lifted one shoulder. "Just threw this on at the last minute."

Nico wore a black T-shirt and black basketball shorts, looking every bit the broad-shouldered, athletically inclined hottie that he was. He'd probably just thrown on the first thing he reached for, but it didn't matter because he was gorgeous in everything.

He lifted her suitcase and attached it in the flatbed next to his, securing them both with crisscrossing bungee cords. She climbed in the passenger side and let out a breath. This was it. The beginning of two weeks of adventurous, fun days and sweaty, lust-filled nights. She squirmed with excitement topped with pure anxiety.

Be bold! Where are you, slutty vixen?

He got in and started the truck. "Ready?"

She swallowed. "Yup."

"I figured we'd go straight through to Cleveland today," he said as he pulled out of the lot. "Try to get some miles down fast. Eight hours and then—" another killer charming smile "—the night is ours."

She got a hot flash, followed quickly by nerves, which, of course, made her even weirder. "What about the Pez Museum? We don't want to miss that."

He glanced over. "Where's that?"

"Pennsylvania."

"I don't have a ton of time for sightseeing. I have to get back in a little less than two weeks to make it to my brother's wedding."

"Oh."

"I'm best man. Well, one of five best men. Vince wanted all of his brothers as best men."

"You have five brothers?"

"Yup. Two biological, three step. My dad married their mom. It all worked out."

"You're so lucky. I'm an only child." Least she'd grown up like one.

"I am lucky."

She hadn't realized they wouldn't have the full two weeks. That meant she had even less time to make this casual, sweaty, lust-filled affair happen. There was no time for nerves. "So how many days do we have?"

"Almost two weeks. Thirteen days."

"Did you know Santa is the bestselling Pez?"

"You can see anything you want in Cleveland."

Drop the Pez. You don't even eat Pez.

"Cleveland has the world's largest rubber stamp," she informed him.

"Yeah? What about the Rock and Roll Hall of Fame?"

She wrinkled her nose. "Too touristy. The rubber stamp is really cool."

"All right. If you say so, but we only have time for one stop."

She nodded and settled in for a lot of hours on the road ahead. Might as well get a jump start on her required listening. "You have a lighter?"

He glanced at her. "No smoking in my truck."

She held up her charger. "It's for my iPhone. I have some lectures I need to listen to. It should work on the radio speakers if I tune it right." He gestured toward it, and she hooked everything up. A few moments later, a voice droned, "Welcome to the New York State Bar Plus Review Course. The lectures are broken down as follows—"

"Lily?"

"Yes?"

The professor's voice droned on. "Crimes, contracts, constitutional law…"

"Do we *both* have to study for the bar exam?" Nico asked.

"Of course not, silly."

The professor continued. "…real property, torts, and civil procedure."

"Don't you have headphones or earbuds or something?" Nico asked.

"No." She smiled. "I thought this way you'd be able to quiz me at the end."

"So we *are* both studying for the bar."

"No, just me. You're going to ask me questions at the end."

More from the professor. "State-specific questions covered at the end of lecture fifty."

Nico groaned.

"I have eight hundred flashcards you can quiz me with too," Lily said, waving toward the flatbed behind them. "In my suitcase."

Nico turned the volume down. "We're getting you headphones."

"Headphones give me a headache. You don't have to listen. Just, you know, think about something else." She turned the volume back up.

The professor went on. "Lecture one…"

Nico groaned even louder.

"Shh!" Lily admonished.

~ ~ ~

Eight long lecture-filled hours later, Nico parked the truck in a municipal lot in Cleveland and rested his forehead on the steering wheel. How in the world did his stepbrother Gabe get through all this boring law stuff? He knew way too much about things that barely made any sense to him. Torts? What the hell was a tort? Eight hours, and they'd only gotten through seven lectures. He couldn't take it. He'd do all the driving, he'd indulge her need to see weird stuff like a giant rubber stamp, but he would *not* study for the bar exam. There was a reason he went straight to work at the garage. He was a hands-on kind of guy. He sucked at academics. He felt like driving a fork into his brain to get rid of all the boring stuff crammed in there.

Lily tapped his shoulder. He raised his head and cocked a brow.

"I booked us at the Hilton," she said.

"Seriously?"

"My dad has free rewards club rooms at a ton of places from all his traveling."

"So all the hotels are high-end and free?" Nico asked. Strange that the wealthy, who could easily afford a room, got them for free, but what the hell. He could deal with living the high life for a bit.

She nodded. "Okay?"

"More than okay. That almost makes up for the massive bar exam headache I have."

She gave his arm a playful smack. "Oh, you do not. That was a very soothing voice."

He did an impersonation of the drone from the recording. "Civil procedure in the state of New York requires...zzz."

She laughed. "Let's check in and grab some dinner."

"Can we get room service?" he asked for the sole purpose of keeping her in the room and getting her naked ASAP.

"Sure. Why not?"

They checked in, and Lily flashed some gold card that immediately got them the VIP treatment.

"Will your dad know I'm with you?" he asked. "From the hotel."

She lowered her voice. "No. He won't even notice I've used the rooms. He never keeps track of his rewards program cards."

That was great with him. The last thing he needed was to piss off his best client. Nico asked the guy behind the counter where they could get earbuds.

Lily frowned. "I don't like earbuds. They feel weird in my ears and give me a headache."

"Torts give me a headache," he said. "Wear them or the Bar Plus Review Course gets it."

She giggled at his mock threatening voice. He loved making her laugh. And that smile just lit up her face. He went to the hotel gift shop and found some headphones that would be more comfortable than the earbuds for her. He met Lily back in the center foyer.

He looked around for their suitcases. "Where's our luggage?"

She waved a hand. "Staff is bringing it up for us."

O-kay. He felt weird not bringing his own suitcase up, but whatever. They headed toward the elevators near the back of the lobby and passed by a sign that read Finkel-Stewart wedding.

"Ooh, a wedding," Lily said.

He had zero interest in weddings. His own at twenty-one had been a big church wedding followed by a reception that his ex's parents had paid for, taking out a loan to afford it. What a waste of money.

They headed upstairs and both ordered room service of steak, mashed potatoes, and mixed vegetables. Someone delivered their luggage a few minutes later. He could get used to this kind of life. While they waited for the food, he crashed on the bed, hoping Lily would join him. They had two queen-size beds, but one of them would not be used if he had anything to say about it. After all that driving to the tune of bar exam lectures, he more than deserved this. They could fool around a bit before dinner, he decided. An appetizer to the main course.

"C'mere," he said in the husky voice that always got results.

Lily was fiddling with her giant suitcase. For some reason she was unpacking and putting things in drawers even though they would only be here for the night. "I'm okay."

"Why're you unpacking? We're leaving first thing in the morning."

"I don't want to live out of a suitcase."

"C'mere. Rest with me before the food comes."

She waved a hand in his direction. "I'm okay."

"Lily."

"Hmm?"

"Are you ever going to look at me?"

She turned and looked at a point somewhere over his shoulder. "Hi." She turned back to lining up a variety of items on the desk. He saw five stacks of flashcards all wrapped in plastic. Hell no.

"I'm not doing those flashcards," he said.

She turned, one pack of cards clutched in her hand. "Just a few?"

"No."

"I'd help you if you were trying to pass the most important exam of your life."

He crossed his arms and pretended to sleep.

She huffed, and he stayed like that until their food arrived. They had a small sitting area in the room with a sofa and coffee table and went there to eat.

"What do you want to do after this?" he asked casually as he sliced off a piece of medium-well sirloin. He hoped the answer was screw your brains out. He watched her for telltale signs of blushing.

"I really want to see that rubber stamp!" she said with a smile and no blush at all.

"Oh. Yeah? What's so special about it?"

"It's the world's largest." She took a sip of Pellegrino sparkling water. "And it says 'FREE' on it. All capital letters."

He scooped up some potatoes. "Oh, well, if it says free in capital letters, of course we have to see it."

She nodded. "We should go right after this before

it gets too dark. It's at the harbor near the Rock and Roll Hall of Fame."

"Do we possibly have time to see the best thing in Cleveland?"

She nodded. "If we hurry."

"I meant the Rock and Roll Hall of Fame." He pulled out his cell and did a search to find their hours. "Nope. Missed it. Rubber stamp it is."

She beamed, and he warmed at the sight, pleased to make her happy. Ah, hell, it was worth it just for that.

A short while later, they arrived at Willard Park, where Nico obligingly snapped a picture of Lily in front of the giant rubber stamp lying on its side.

She ran to look at the picture and then told him the meaning behind the free, which was intended to point to the freedom of slaves, as it was originally located across from the Civil War Soldiers and Sailors Monument, which made a helluva lot more sense. It was getting dark, so rubber stamp duly noted, they headed back to the hotel.

He snagged her hand as they walked and tucked it in his. He had to get her used to his touch if he was going to make any progress tonight. She didn't look at him, just kept walking a little stiffly. Nerves, he figured.

"I remembered what you said," he told her.

"About the slow stuff."

She jolted. "Oh. Uh-huh." She walked faster. He kept up, keeping her hand tucked in his. She must be as eager as he was to get tonight started. It was all he could think about all week.

They arrived at the hotel lobby to the sound of a DJ blasting music from the nearby ballroom where the wedding was being held.

Lily stopped short and looked up at him. "I'm the plus one of the groom's cousin. You're the plus one of the bride's cousin."

"What?"

"I feel like dancing. Come on!" She opened the ballroom door and pulled him into the dimly lit room, where wedding guests were getting down to "Love Shack" by the B-52s. Old school. He dragged his feet. He wasn't exactly dressed for a wedding. Lily was in a dress. He was in a T-shirt and shorts.

She went to the edge of the dance floor and started dancing crazy. Her arms swung up and down as she alternated hip wiggles that brought her down low and popped up. He found himself smiling. She grabbed his hand and pulled him with her.

"Lil, I'm not dressed for a wedding."

She held up a finger and left him standing there. He nodded to a curious grandma type dancing nearby. Lily returned with a suit jacket and tie.

"Where'd you get this?" he asked as she wrapped the tie around his neck. She did a sloppy, loose knot.

"Someone left it at a table."

He held the jacket out in front of him. Too small. He shook his head and put it back on the table. Lily pulled at him again and started her crazy dance. He could only watch in astonished amusement. She did like to dance.

"Come on!" she hollered, dancing all around him. "Shake that thing, Marino!"

He shifted back and forth on his feet. He could do two dances—a slow dance and a waltz thanks to the ballroom dance lessons he and his brothers were forced to take before their dad married their stepmom.

"More!" she said, bumping her hip against him.

He grabbed her by the hips, maneuvering her in front of him for a slow dance. He moved them slowly side to side. The song changed to a slow one, which would've been perfect, except the dance floor cleared, making them stick out even more. He was about to leave when Lily wrapped her arms around his neck.

He leaned down toward her ear. "As much as I like slow dancing with you, maybe we should take this upstairs."

"There's no music upstairs."

"I'll sing for you."

She pulled back to look in his eyes. "You're

funny."

"Thank you." Except he was serious. He really needed this upstairs thing to happen soon. Having Lily's curves so close was like a tease, luring him in for more. A lot more than could happen on the dance floor of a wedding they were crashing.

"No," she said.

"No?"

"I want to dance here." She pressed closer, her breasts against his chest, and he found it tough to refuse her. Also, he was rock hard and needed some cover for the tent in his basketball shorts.

"Lily," he said in a low voice, "people are starting to stare. I'm sure they noticed I'm in shorts and a tie."

"Just keep dancing," she hissed.

He did. Lily was very different from any woman he'd ever been with, and he was starting to get into that. The song ended and an older man in a tuxedo approached.

"Time to go," Lily said, grabbing his hand. They ran out the door, laughing.

~ ~ ~

Lily loved crashing weddings and it had the added benefit of giving her more time to get over her nerves at what she knew Nico expected of her tonight. What she wanted, really, if she could just stop getting so worked up over all the ways she'd disappoint him. She set her shoes in the corner of the hotel room and took the ruby-wine-colored satin babydoll she'd bought just for this special event out of her suitcase. She tossed her purse over her shoulder because some of her favorite makeup was in there and turned to find Nico lying in bed, wearing nothing but black boxer briefs and a seductive smile. Her heart pounded. Omigod. He looked like a freaking underwear model, all olive skin and muscles. There was literally not an ounce of fat on him anywhere.

So she did what any sane woman would do when faced with such manly perfection—

She hid in the bathroom.

For a *really* long time.

Sure, she was all big talk (thank you, inner slutty vixen!), and he'd sworn to take things slow, but now that she was at the Big Moment, she was in a near panic. She couldn't possibly compare to the type of women he must be used to. Like that Tiffany he'd mistaken her for because of her red hair.

She changed into the babydoll nightie in the bathroom and reapplied makeup, and even though the nightie looked great, she couldn't bear to have him touch her in it. The nightie looked good precisely because it was loose and flowing. The moment his hands touched her waist, he'd feel her plumpness, her much too soft belly. When they'd been dancing earlier, she'd been careful to stay close enough that his hands would rest on her back. If only she'd had more than a week to work out. Doing twenty stomach crunches a day had shown zero results.

She sat on the toilet lid and started a game of solitaire on her cell phone. Maybe if she stalled long enough, he'd fall asleep. Four games in, Nico called through the door.

"You okay in there?"

"Almost ready," she caroled back.

Half an hour later…

"Lil?" he called.

It was kinda cute the way he called her Lil.

"Yes, Nic?" she asked, trying out a nickname of her own.

His voice rumbled close through the locked bathroom door. "What's wrong?"

"Nothing."

"Are you sick?"

"No, I'm just getting ready."

"Still?"

"You can go to sleep if you'd like. I'll be out when I'm finished."

He grumbled something she didn't quite catch, and she returned to her seventh winning game of solitaire.

Another half an hour later…

Her eyes were drooping now. It had been a very long day and her nerves had further worn her down. It was very quiet in the room. She hoped that meant he'd fallen asleep. She stashed her phone in her purse and quietly opened the door, coming face to face with Nico.

"Hi," he said.

"Hi!" she squeaked.

He reached for her waist, and she jumped back, slamming the door in his face.

"Lil," he said through the door, "I won't bite."

She laughed heartily, all confidence. "I know that."

"Then why're you hiding in the bathroom?"

"I'm not." She should probably take out her contacts. She did that, and the world went fuzzy. She put on her round wire-framed glasses so she wouldn't trip on the way out. Well, now she didn't have to worry at all. Nico would take one look at her professor glasses and be completely turned off.

She yawned very loudly. "Could you step back from the door?"

"I'm back."

She opened the door to find him three feet away. She dodged past him, hurried to the still-made bed on the far side of the room, banged her shin on the corner of the bedframe, and dove under the covers. *Ouch.* She set her glasses on the nightstand and settled on her side, giving him her back. She let out a very unladylike snore for good measure.

The bed creaked and the covers lifted as he joined her. She tensed.

His warm hand rested on her upper arm. "I know you're not asleep that quickly."

She looked at him over her shoulder. "I'm supertired from all that driving. You are too. Eight hours is a long day of traveling. Goodnight."

"Goodnight? That's it?"

She fake snored again.

He let out a noisy breath.

She scrunched her eyes shut tight and tried to think soothing thoughts because having him so close, the heat of his superhot body warming her back, was making her a nervous wreck. She'd never get to sleep with him next to her. She was about to ask him to move when he stroked her hair.

"Am I not smoking hot anymore?" he asked.

She giggled at that ridiculous question and looked at him over her shoulder. There was just enough light from the streetlight outside that she could see his smile. "You're still smoking hot, and you know it."

"How about a goodnight kiss?"

Her whole body vibrated with nerves and anticipation. A kiss. She could handle a kiss. She rolled over. "I'll kiss you."

"Okay."

He lay flat on his back, waiting. Oh. So she was the aggressor here. Her nerves vanished in light of this new unexpected situation. He did have very kissable lips. She leaned over him and placed a soft kiss on his lips. He tasted minty, his lips like warm velvet. He didn't grab her or anything, so she kept going, deepening the kiss, darting her tongue in to touch his. His large hand slid into her hair, holding her there. It felt so good that she forgot about being nervous and kept going. So much deliciousness, so much beautiful chest. Her hand stroked over his chest hair, his pecs, across his ribs. A soft moan came out. Hers. His hand left her hair and stroked lower, down her back. She broke the kiss and quickly scooted away.

"Goodnight," she said, turning on her side away from him.

"Are you really that tired?" he asked, his voice rumbling close in her ear.

She could feel the heat of him again, so close she felt like a live wire, all jittery and electric. Crazy nerves and an overpowering lust battled it out within her. Her heart raced.

"Yes," she said. "Very, very tired."

His voice was gentle now. "Sure you're not just…I dunno…nervous for some reason?"

She snored.

"Lil?"

More snoring.

"How many guys have you been with?" he asked.

Omigod, she was not answering that question. One guy sounded so pathetic. He would definitely think something was wrong with her.

"How many?" he pressed.

"You really don't want to know," she replied. "Goodnight."

"I really do."

Snore.

"Am I your first?" he asked.

She snorted. "No." At least she could proudly claim she wasn't a twenty-five-year-old virgin. If one could be proud of that.

"Second?" he asked.

Snore.

"I take that as a yes," he said. "That's okay. I told you I'd go slow."

She rolled over and met his deep brown eyes that were full of sympathy and understanding, which made her feel ten times worse. "For your information, I've been with lots of guys. Way more than one." In her imagination. "So don't act all superior. We both know you've had your share of women." She flopped back over, miffed at the reminder.

"Are you seriously mad right now?" he asked. "I wasn't acting superior at all."

"Yes, you were, with all your questions and your sympathy eyes." Her throat got tight. "So just think about all those other women if it makes you feel better."

He groaned. "It doesn't make me feel better at all. Lil, come on. I don't have sympathy eyes. They're just regular."

"Goodnight," she said with a tone of finality.

He flopped onto his back with a groan, making the mattress bounce. She blinked rapidly, feeling like a complete and total loser, but unable to make things better. She just couldn't compete with all those women. A short while later, he left the bed, and she heard the shower running.

Having the bed to herself didn't make her feel any better. What was she doing? This was supposed to be her big sex tutorial. The new Lily. But somehow the old Lily was stomping all over her confidence. She couldn't sleep. She had to fix this somehow. Be brave and forward. Maybe they should've ordered some wine. Something to get over this awkward, nervous tension that made her feel frozen.

She heard the shower turn off and a short while later Nico got into the other bed. She told herself to move. Just get up, walk over, and join him. It wasn't that hard to do. He'd said he'd go slow. But would he think she was too big, too solid, too Godzilla-like? Would he recoil from her soft poochy stomach?

She bit her lip. *Stop it*, she told herself. *This is why you're here. Get up!*

She slipped out of bed, crossed the short distance between the two beds and looked down at him. He was sprawled out on his stomach, lightly snoring.

She couldn't wake him. Not after he'd driven all day today. She slipped back into bed, torn between relief and disappointment. Tomorrow night, she promised herself.

CHAPTER EIGHT

Nico left Cleveland determined that today would end in a much better situation than blue balls for him. He knew Lily must be inexperienced, but he didn't care about that. He just wanted to be with her so bad. When she'd come out of the bathroom last night in that skimpy red lingerie, it took everything he had not to just grab her and take her against the wall. She was sexy as all hell, and the fact that she didn't know it made her even more appealing. She wasn't playing games with him or putting on a performance like a lot of his past lovers. She was just genuine. And she'd been just as into that kiss as he was. He could do slow. What he absolutely could not do was nothing.

He'd sooner drive back to Connecticut than spend another night with her prancing around in that tiny satin thing, her breasts nearly popping out the top, while he tossed and turned. That kind of torture was too much to ask any man. He'd had to sleep in the other bed, for crying out loud. He couldn't take being that close and not touching.

He glanced over at her in a V-neck T-shirt that showed off her cleavage and her shorts that showed plenty of curvy, smooth leg. He liked this outfit even better than the dress she had on yesterday because there was so much more leg. She always had her cleavage on display. He liked that about her. She wore large round shades, so he couldn't read her expression at all. Was she still mad about his questions last night? Embarrassed? He wished he knew so he could smooth things over. Hooking up wasn't a big deal at all, and if he could just get her past her nerves, he was sure they'd have a lot of fun together.

He waved a hand near her face to get her attention since she had the headphones on, already listening to the bar exam lecture. At least he didn't have that torture.

She pulled one side of the headphones away from her ear. "What?"

"You want coffee and donuts?"

"Just coffee."

"This'll be a short drive today," he told her. "Just five hours to Chicago. I don't want you tired out tonight."

"Oh," she chirped. "I don't mind a long drive. We can go further than that."

"Chicago," he said firmly. Besides, he was supposed to meet Luke for dinner. His brother traveled to Chicago and London a lot on business.

She put her headphones back in place and sank lower in the seat. Was it really so awful to be with him? Geez, he was starting to feel like the Big Bad Wolf. He never had to work this hard to get a woman naked.

A short while later, he had two coffees and a couple of glazed donuts. Both the donuts were for him. He was hungry after spending an hour in the hotel's workout room this morning, trying to get rid of some of the tension from his restless night. He'd woken up off and on all night, listening to Lily sighing and breathing heavy in her sleep, thinking about her soft skin and sweet scent. He took a sip of coffee and then a big bite of donut.

Lily watched him hungrily. He held out the donut. "Wanna bite?"

She shook her head and sipped her coffee. He took another bite, and she still watched. He handed it to her, and she ate it quickly, like she was starving. Now why did she say no to a donut in the first place? He shook his head and pulled the second donut from the bag and ate that one.

She pulled the headphones off and stopped the recording. "Thanks."

"Sure," he replied. "Anything special you want to do in Chicago? We'll have all afternoon and night. I heard the Navy Pier is supposed to be cool."

She licked the glaze from the donut off her fingers—that pink tongue through those plump pink lips—kill him now. He really wished he hadn't seen that. She smiled over at him.

He grimaced.

"Are you okay?" she asked.

"Yup."

"I really want to see President Obama's barber's chair. It's preserved in Plexiglas at the place he used to get his haircut."

Of course it was. "Really? No shopping, no museums, no Navy Pier? Just a barber chair?"

"It was the president's, Nico. That's special." And with that, she put her headphones on and started listening to that awful droning voice again.

He turned on the radio, thankful for the music that was so much better than studying for the bar exam. He glanced at her cleavage again, her soft legs stretched out in front of her, and restrained himself mightily from touching. Soon. He could wait a little longer. A short drive, a quick look at a barber chair, and then she'd be all his.

~ ~ ~

Lily had been to Chicago before, but Nico hadn't, so after they checked out the barber chair, which looked exactly like a regular barber chair (in Plexiglas), but was extra special for being the president's, she made sure they did a long walking tour, where she pointed out famous sights in an effort to wear him out. She pointed and talked a lot without stopping anywhere. Museum of Science and Industry! Millennium Park! Lake Michigan! Nico listened attentively, frequently asking if she wanted to stop and look at any of the sights, which, of course, she didn't, she had to keep him moving. After that, she took him shopping at the department stores on Michigan Avenue, which would wear most men out.

Nico held her purse while she tried on tons of outfits. Guilt over her nefarious intentions and terrible nerves kept her from buying anything. Because how could she enjoy herself when her sole purpose was to wear Nico out?

It wasn't that he wasn't the most gorgeous sexy man on the planet. He was, he definitely was. And he was being so nice and patient with her. It was her. She was the problem. She knew it and was embarrassed by it, but there was nothing she could do. She simply had to put him off until Las Vegas, where she hoped they'd both get so drunk it would be easy. He wouldn't remember anything except that they'd done the deed.

Once they got over that hurdle, she could finally relax. Maybe.

She emerged from the Bloomingdale's dressing room empty-handed. It was the third department store she'd toured in four hours.

"I'm beginning to suspect you're not planning on buying anything," he said.

"I didn't like the fit," she said. "You want to go to a bar?"

He handed over her purse, settling the strap over her shoulder. "We should have dinner first."

"Let's just get crazy and get drunk," she said. Because she could get drunk in Chicago just as easily as Las Vegas. Why wait?

He slung an arm over her shoulders and tapped her nose with one finger. "Now why would I do that? I want to remember everything about our night."

She swallowed hard. "Oh."

"We have to get deep-dish pizza in Chicago, right?"

She nodded, unable to speak when he was this close, smiling down at her. He was breathtaking.

"My stepbrother Luke's in town," he said, guiding her out the door. "He texted me he knows a place not far from here. Follow me."

"We're meeting your brother?"

"Yeah. Is that a problem?"

"I guess not. I just didn't think we'd be meeting each other's families."

"Just Luke."

He walked with his arm around her shoulders like it was the most natural thing in the world. She was burning up with the closeness, the casualness of the gesture at odds with the fact that she, Lily Spencer, had the most amazing man right here interested in her. At least temporarily. Two weeks, no strings. That was their deal.

"Luke's the one that set me up with the redheaded Tiffany," he said.

She grimaced. "Only you got me."

"I got you."

"Do you wish you were here with Tiffany?"

He leaned down and kissed the tip of her nose. "I thought I was with Tiffany. Who are you again?"

She smacked his chest, and he laughed. A short walk later, they stopped in front of the restaurant, Gino's East. A man with dirty blond hair leaned against the brick building, staring at his cell phone.

Nico stopped in front of him. "Hey."

The man looked up and smiled, almost a smirk as he took them both in. Her breath caught. Was Nico's entire family this gorgeous? That face would've been more than enough to make any woman swoon—dirty blond hair cropped short, dark blue eyes, neatly trimmed beard and mustache, and a sexy smirk. But he was also tall and muscular and radiated confidence.

"You must be Lily," he said. "I'm Luke."

"So nice to meet you," she breathed. "I'm Lily Spencer."

Nico gave her a look, eyes narrowed. "Maybe we should go in."

"Spencer," Luke said. "Is your dad George Spencer?"

She cringed. He knew her family. Now he'd treat her differently, no casual joking around or fun. "Yup."

Luke turned to Nico. "She's the Spencer heiress. Did you know? You just said the redhead."

She turned to Nico. "Just the redhead? Couldn't remember my name?"

Nico scowled at Luke. "I told you her name. Of course I know her dad. He's my client. Can we eat?"

Luke held the door open and gestured for them to go inside. She'd never been here before. The walls and booths and even some of the chairs were covered in graffiti. The tables were covered with red and white checked tablecloths. So fun!

After a short wait, they were shown to a booth. Nico grabbed her hand and pulled her into the booth next to him. They ordered a deep-dish Gino's supreme with sausage that the server said would take forty-five minutes to cook. The brothers each got a beer. Lily got a glass of Chianti. Nico and Luke talked about their other brother Vince's upcoming wedding, the Red Sox, and a long complicated analysis of Luke's Porsche, which he said was making a strange noise at idle. Lily didn't mind. She loved the easy banter and conversation between the brothers. Like they were best friends. She'd longed for a family bond like that her whole life.

"So, Lily, sorry to blather on about my car," Luke said after they'd been served the pizza. "Let's talk about you. What are your intentions toward my brother?"

She laughed, and Nico scowled. "Honorable, sir."

Luke smiled. "Good, good. I hope you intend to make an honest man out of him after your two-week—" he lowered his voice to a husky tone "—road trip."

"Shut up," Nico told Luke. "What're you doing in town anyway?"

"My company's moving a department from Chicago to New York, and they want me to help with the transition," he said. "I'm a financial planner," he told Lily. "You ever need someone to help you invest—"

"Drop it," Nico snapped.

Luke inclined his head. "So what've you two been up to today?"

"Shopping," Lily said.

Luke raised a brow and took a bite of pizza.

"Among other things," Nico said. "Just the usual touristy stuff."

"You do Navy Pier?" Luke asked. "The Ferris wheel gives you a fantastic view of the skyline and the lake. You should check it out."

"Maybe we will," Nico said.

"We might be too busy," Lily said. She kinda had a thing about Ferris wheels.

Nico smiled widely and put his arm around her. "We might be too busy."

"Or not," Lily added, suddenly realizing a trip to the pier could prolong the night and his inevitable disappointment with her in bed later.

Luke just took a long pull on his beer, watching them both. She had a feeling he was as sharp as Nico. She just hoped he didn't bring up anything embarrassing like the fact that Nico couldn't wait to get back to the hotel, and she could wait forever.

After a delicious dinner, where she managed not to spill any sauce, Lily got a pen from her purse and added her initials to the small bit of back booth that hadn't been graffitied.

"Don't forget to put Nico's initials," Luke said. "And a little four. You know, for-ever."

"You're asking for it," Nico growled.

Lily flushed. "You want me to add your initials?" she asked Nico.

Nico glanced at her, his gaze dropping to her mouth. "Don't worry about it," he said in a low voice. A stab of disappointment went through her, but then he took her hand and held it, which made her feel a little better.

Luke insisted on paying, putting it on his corporate account, and they headed outside. Luke still had to check into his hotel and said he had some work he needed to do before tomorrow, so they said their goodbyes.

"Well, Lily Spencer, it was wonderful to meet you," Luke said as he took her hand and held it between both of his. "I hope we see you at Sunday family dinner. My mom would love you. She makes these delicious cookies."

She flushed. "Oh! Well. That's very nice—"

"No Sunday dinner," Nico said as he put a palm on Luke's face and pushed him back. "No cookies either."

Lily's cheeks burned. It was like Nico had just told Luke they were hooking up and nothing more. "Nice to meet you," she said, backing away from both men.

"Until we meet again," Luke said with a sly smile.

Nico socked him in the shoulder. The brothers traded some low words she couldn't quite hear, and then Luke left with a laugh.

Nico appeared at her side and took her hand. "You want to check out Navy Pier or go back to the hotel?"

"Let's check out the pier!" she chirped.

He held her hand as they walked. She was still getting used to all this touchy-feely stuff.

"We should do the Ferris wheel," Nico said. "I'll bet the skyline looks cool at sunset."

And because he'd been so accommodating with all of her shopping and not buying anything, and because, more than anything, she wanted to delay tonight's embarrassing, awkward, maybe seduction, she agreed.

It was a good half-hour walk to the pier, and their hotel, the Talbott, was back where they'd been shopping near Michigan Avenue, so Lily figured all the walking would not only work off all the delicious pizza, but also wear them both out.

As they approached the pier, she tried not to look up at the giant wheel of death. There was a slight breeze coming up off Lake Michigan. If the wind kicked up any harder, it would rock the Ferris wheel car and tip them right out. Her heart kicked up a notch.

By the time they stood in line for tickets, her palms were sweaty, and she had to pull her hand out of Nico's to wipe it on the front of her shorts. He took that opportunity to check his cell for messages, and she took the opportunity to move a few steps away, drop her head between her knees, and take a few deep breaths. *You can do this. You've been on a Ferris wheel before.*

Last time she'd thrown up.

Whatever. She straightened, still a little light-headed. She didn't want to ruin this for Nico.

"Got it," he said, five short minutes later, holding up the tickets. "Let's get in line."

She hoped it was a very, very long line.

It wasn't.

"I'll bet at the top we'll get some nice pictures of the skyline and the lake," he said.

"Yup," she said tightly.

"You okay? You look a little pale."

She shook her head and pinched some color back in her cheeks. "Just a little tired. Busy day."

He slid an arm around her shoulders. "We'll go back to the hotel right after this, okay?"

AAAAH!!!!

"Okay," she said.

He tipped her chin up and kissed her gently. She calmed considerably, as all her focus was on that kiss and not her freaky fear of heights. She really, really liked his kisses.

Before she knew it, they were boarding one of the cars of death. It swung precariously as the previous riders, a father and his toddler son, got off. She felt a little light-headed. Do *not* pass out.

Nico guided her in with a hand on the small of her back and followed behind her. The door was latched shut, like *that* would prevent them from tipping out. One gust of wind and they were pancakes on the pier. She clicked the seatbelt and prayed.

The wheel started at a slow lift and then they were airborne. She began a frantic bargaining with God. *If I survive this, I will give up chocolate.* The wind picked up, and they swayed gently. She squeezed her eyes shut. *I will dedicate myself to helping the homeless. I will crochet one hundred blankets a week for—*

"Lily?"

For every man, woman, and child that has ever felt chilly.

"Hey, Lil, why're your eyes closed? You're missing the view."

She kept her eyes scrunched tight. Her stomach dropped as they lifted even higher. Their car swung slightly in the breeze. *I will adopt every dog that needs a home on the East Coast. Even the yappy ones.*

"Open your eyes," Nico said. "Check out the sunset."

"It's quite nice," she said, eyes closed.

"What's the matter?" he asked.

"I'm afraid of heights," she whispered in case the Ferris wheel overheard and decided to tip her out. The wheel stopped. She opened her eyes and quickly shut them again. Oh, God. They were going to be stuck like this at the tippy-top. Maybe it malfunctioned.

"Why'd you get on a Ferris wheel, then?" Nico asked.

"Because I want to *not* be afraid of heights," she said. It was true. She was trying to face more of her fears head-on. Except for the spider thing. And snakes. And clowns. She shuddered, thinking of them.

Nico wrapped his arm around her. "I got you. Open your eyes."

"Sure, you got me, but who's got you? This thing could tip with the slightest movement."

"You know what's good to do at the top of the Ferris wheel?" he asked in a low, husky voice that temporarily distracted her.

"What?"

"Make out."

"Oh. Really?" She'd never heard that before and briefly wondered if he was making it up, but then he was kissing her. She slowly unclenched from her frozen state. His warm hand cupped her face, his mouth was hot and demanding, and she was quickly overwhelmed. He kept going, his tongue thrusting inside her mouth, and she melted against him, the kiss heightened by their imminent death.

He pulled back and smiled. "Now look."

She did. The skyline was spectacular with the Willis Tower prominently highlighted by the setting sun.

Nico took his arm off her, and the car lurched with the movement.

"What're you doing?" she screeched.

He pulled his cell out of his shorts pocket. "I want to take a picture."

"Oh."

And then he took a picture of her.

"What're you taking a picture of me for? I thought you wanted the skyline."

He gazed at her and there was no sympathy in those eyes, only warmth. "I wanted a picture of courage."

A slow smile formed on her lips. "Thank you."

The Ferris wheel started moving again. "Whoa!" she yelped.

Nico's arm settled around her shoulders. "You got this."

And she did. She kept her eyes open the entire time and stayed very, very still. She felt like kissing the ground when she finally got off the wheel of death. Her legs were shaky, but Nico's hand was once again strong and firm, holding hers.

They walked back to the hotel and gradually her legs stopped feeling like rubber.

He squeezed her hand as they stepped inside the hotel foyer. "You're not hiding in the bathroom all night again, are you?"

Her cheeks burned. "I wasn't hiding."

"Yes, you were."

She shook her head, acting annoyed when she was really just mortified at how easily he saw through her. Once they got into the hotel room, she grabbed her pajamas and toiletry bag and headed for the bathroom.

"I'm coming to get you if you take too long," he warned.

"Nico, I need some privacy."

"Oh. Sorry."

She went inside and locked the door. Her inner slutty vixen had permanently deserted her. The bitch. A moment later she heard the TV and relaxed a bit. It was time for the big guns. They were, unfortunately, both sober and there was no way she could pull this sexy temptress thing off. No lingerie tonight. Contacts out, glasses on. T-shirt and sweatpants to bed like she always wore. The outfit was boxy and shapeless and oh so comfortable. Nico would realize she was nothing to get excited about and then they could both relax and watch TV before going to sleep. She took a few deep breaths, opened the door, and faced him. He'd been waiting for her, standing just outside the bathroom door, in his blue boxer briefs. Her very own underwear model. He had no clue how intimidating it was to be this close to someone this sexy.

One corner of his mouth lifted. "Nice glasses, professor."

"Thank you."

He slid them off and set them on the bathroom counter. Then he pulled her out of the bathroom. His hand cupped her jaw as he slowly leaned down and brushed his mouth over hers. Her eyes drifted shut, and she let out a small sigh as he kissed her into a nearly drunken state, all loose-limbed, melty, and light-headed. Then he was kissing her and maneuvering her until she felt the cool wall at her back. She relaxed a little because it wasn't the bed. His kiss turned more urgent, hot and intense, as he pressed his hard body against hers. She tore her mouth from his, suddenly realizing he could do a lot against the wall that he could do in bed. He immediately went for her neck, kissing her, tasting her, his teeth scraping against her. Her knees buckled, and she clung to him. He returned to her mouth, kissing her hard and deep, the heat and strength of his body pressing against hers making her forget her nerves and simply surrender.

After a gloriously long time of deep kisses that took her breath away, he stopped, took her hand, and tugged her toward the bed. She didn't move. He returned to her and kissed her again. She pulled away.

Her body and brain battled it out—*keep going, stop, keep going, stop.* If only she knew for sure she wouldn't disappoint him.

"What's wrong?" he asked, his voice rough. His heated gaze pinned her with unwavering intensity. She swallowed hard and looked away as nerves gripped her again.

A beat passed in silence.

"I have a headache from the headphones," she finally said, meeting his eyes again. "From the bar exam lecture this morning," she added, waving a hand in the air at the puzzled expression on his face. "You know, on the ride in."

"You do not."

"I told you those things give me a headache."

"Then I'll get you some Tylenol."

"I just need a good night's sleep. Goodnight, Nico."

"Lil, I know you feel this—" he gestured back and forth between them "—this chemistry we have."

She bit her lip and turned, walking around to the far side of the bed.

"Just tell me what the problem is so I can fix it," he said.

That was just it. He couldn't fix it. She shook her head and climbed into bed, pretending to sleep. He was silent for a long moment; then he went into the bathroom and shut the door. A few minutes later, she heard the shower.

She shut her eyes tight as a tear slipped out. Dammit. So much for courage.

CHAPTER NINE

Nico had never been so close to a woman for so many hours and days and nights and not gotten naked. This was a brand-new experience for him, all the driving and sharing meals and hotel rooms, with their clothes on. He wasn't so sure it was a good thing.

He glanced over at the temptress sitting on the other side of the truck, headphones on as she listened to even more bar exam crap. He'd thought she was beautiful before, but now that he knew her better, all her quirky, brave ways, he was getting in deep. He thought about her nearly all night before he mercifully crashed into sleep. Replaying their day, remembering everything she said or did, trying to figure her out. He was falling for her, like he'd only fallen once in his life with his ex-wife, and it was damn uncomfortable.

No, he knew better than to let it get that far. He just needed to sleep with her, get her out of his system so to speak, so he could stop thinking about her so much. The way she wore these T-shirts that he could clearly see her breasts straining against the fabric. The way she melted against him when he kissed her, yet pushed him away when he tried for more. The way she'd so bravely faced her fear of heights head-on. The sweet way she had of looking up at him like he hung the moon.

He was getting sappy. That wasn't him. He wasn't sentimental or mushy at all.

She let out a soft sigh, her lips parting, and he realized she'd fallen asleep. Of course she had, they were halfway to Omaha and the professor droning in her ears would've put anyone to sleep. They were in Iowa with three more hours to go, and he figured he'd let her sleep. Then she'd have no excuse of being too tired or too headachy tonight. She'd feel wide awake, and he'd make good use of that energy. Geez, he only had eleven more days with her. The last day they'd be going their separate ways, so he couldn't count that one. He had to get things moving in the right direction soon before he died of blue balls.

A short while later, she woke with a start. She sat up and pulled the headphones off. "Where are we? Did I miss it?"

"Iowa. Miss what?"

"The second largest collection of salt and pepper shakers, world's largest concrete gnome, Iowa's largest frying pan, take your pick!"

He raised a brow. "Do I have to?"

"We can't miss everything!"

"I don't think I can stop. We've got a lot of miles to cover. I need to get to L.A. and back in time for my brother's wedding."

"Nico, it's Iowa. We *have* to stop."

"We don't *have* to." So far, all he'd seen was cornfields and flat empty land. And he really was on a deadline here. He had to be back in time for the rehearsal dinner.

"I've never been to Iowa, have you?" she asked.

"No."

"Then it's settled. Let me just look it up." Then a few minutes later, "Okay, we're only thirty miles to the second largest collection of salt and pepper shakers."

He groaned. "It's not even the first largest. Seriously?"

"There's more than sixteen thousand of them! And I'm not just talking plain old shakers, I'm talking ceramic cows, Betty Boop, race cars, everything!"

"Well, if there's race cars," he said sarcastically.

"I know, right?"

He couldn't put a damper on her enthusiasm. It was refreshing to find someone so eager, so open to life experiences even when they terrified her. So why was she so cautious with him?

And then it occurred to him that maybe she'd had a bad experience, or, he stiffened with rage, an unwanted one. He didn't want to bring it up, but the rage building in him just at the idea of someone hurting her pushed the words right out.

"Lil, you, uh, have a bad experience with a guy before? Maybe someone who forced themselves on you?" His jaw clenched. He'd kill him. He'd hunt him down and kill him with his bare hands.

He glanced at her to find her jaw dropped. "Did you?" he prompted.

"No. Why do you ask?"

"Because you turn me down every night." There. He put it out there.

"I told you I was tired that one night."

"Yeah, I know. And the headache. Are you going to be tired or have a headache tonight?"

"This conversation is giving me a headache."

"Is there anything I can do to make this easier for you?"

"I'm fine."

He wasn't. He was beginning to think she didn't want to sleep with him at all, which had never happened. Maybe they should get separate hotel rooms. He didn't care what it cost. He couldn't sleep with her nearby every night, prancing around in busty

T-shirts with no bra, taunting him with loose sweatpants that looked like they were about to fall off any minute. He just couldn't take it. No red-blooded man could.

~ ~ ~

Nico pushed the speed limit as they drove through Iowa while Lily kept hollering directions for some town called Traer, where she insisted they had to stop to check out those damn salt and pepper shakers. And how long was that going to take? Sixteen thousand shakers? And he just bet she'd want a picture next to every one.

"Nico, please? It's really important to me."

"Why?"

"Because I want to see America."

"You're just trying to drag out this drive." After two restless nights and more than a week of blue balls, Nico's usual easy charm was slipping. The irony of needing that charm more than ever was not lost on him.

"Can't wait to get to Omaha, huh?" she asked.

"Yes."

"Why?"

He hesitated. Should he admit he wanted nothing more than to get her to the hotel and rip her clothes off? No way. That was as far from a slow seduction as you could get. He glanced over at her, sitting in a white T-shirt with Earth Defense Group emblazoned across her full breasts. He could clearly see her lacy, pushup bra through the thin white fabric. He hoped she hadn't packed any more white T-shirts. She was pure temptation.

"I've heard good things about Omaha," he said tightly.

"Like what?"

"Like…" What had he heard about Omaha? Then he remembered a commercial he saw once. "Like Mutual of Omaha."

"You want to visit an insurance company?"

"Among other things." Like our hotel room, the bed, your body.

"Okay, but first we really need to hit Traer. They even have a winding staircase that leads to nowhere." He looked over, and she beamed. "Right in the middle of the sidewalk!"

He caved. It was that beaming smile. He loved seeing her so happy. "Okay, but we can't stay too long. I have a timetable."

"Okay, okay."

It became clear to Nico an hour into their salt and pepper museum visit that Lily hadn't really listened about his timetable. She was lingering at each display like they had all freaking day. He kept moving her along, and she kept finding one more treasure.

She turned to him. "Ah! Here they are! Betty Boop! Get my picture!"

Nico obligingly took a picture as Lily posed one hand on her hip, eyes wide, lips pursed in an impression of Betty Boop. His body immediately reacted to those pursed lips. Before he could pull her close to sneak a kiss, she raced off to see more.

"A cow," she mouthed to him across the room.

A reluctant smile tugged at his lips.

She appeared at his side and smiled up at him. "Admit it, this is fun."

He put an arm around her and pulled her flush against him. "We really need to get back on the road."

"Cowboy boots!" she exclaimed, moving across the room from him.

He checked his cell while he waited for Lily to take in every freaking set in a glass-fronted china cabinet. He had a text from Luke: *How's our redhead?*

He glanced over to where Lily was bending over, peering into the back of the china cabinet, her curvy ass in shorts making his shorts feel two sizes too small. He turned away and texted back: *Fine.*

A reply came back a few minutes later while he was leaning against the wall as far as he could get from Lily in an effort to cool off. *Just fine?*

Yes.

I thought road trip was code for holing up in a hotel

room for dirty deeds.

Nico shifted, uncomfortably aware of the lack of dirty deeds. *We're in Iowa.*

I heard they're extra dirty there.

All you think about is getting laid.

Sounds like someone's not getting any. Sucker.

That pissed him off. *Fuck you.*

Ha. Mom rented you a tux. Vince says you'd better be at his bachelor party.

Nico didn't reply. He wanted to hook up with Lily for as many nights as possible. And, of course, the whole point of the trip was the car. He shoved a hand in his hair. What was he doing? Wandering through Iowa, not getting any tail, letting his brother down.

He texted back. *I'll be there.* The bachelor party was two nights before the wedding. He'd cut the trip short, put in a lot of miles.

But then he looked up, and Lily was heading straight toward him, a big smile lighting up her face, her curvy hips mesmerizing him with their sway.

Maybe, he quickly added to the text.

"Come see these Victorian boot shakers," she said, and he followed without any protest at all.

Shit. He was in trouble.

~ ~ ~

Once they arrived in Omaha after a lovely three-hour

trip to the salt and pepper shaker museum, Lily took them to Little Italy because she really, really needed to see the fifteen-foot-tall metal fork with pasta. It stood straight up like it had grown out of the sidewalk.

Nico got into that one, posing with it and pretending to eat pasta.

"See, this is good stuff we're seeing on the road," she said.

"Go stand next to it. I want your picture."

She did and pretended to be pulling the fork out of the ground with superhuman strength.

"Now stick your tongue out like you're about to slurp it up," he said.

"That would be more like this," she said, pursing her lips together and pretending to slurp.

He groaned and snapped the picture. "Lil, let's go check in at the hotel. *Please.*"

"We're in Little Italy. Let's eat."

"I'm not hungry."

"You have to be. We had lunch ages ago."

He took her hand. "We'll get room service."

"Come on." She guided him down the street where they found a cute little place with dark wood tables and Tuscan landscape paintings on the walls. They ordered spaghetti and meatballs and shared garlic bread.

Nico was kind of tense. Gone were the charming

smiles and good-natured banter. She was getting tense as a result. Of course she always got more tense the closer it came to hotel time. But they should be in Vegas in two days, where she was sure they'd both get drunk enough to hook up for a forgettable night without any awkwardness involved. Decision made, she smiled sweetly across the table at him.

His return look was so heated it made her squirm. He had no idea what he was getting with her. He'd have to think of a hotter past lover and the thought of that made her burn with humiliation.

By the time they got back to the hotel, she had her excuse ready. She emerged from the bathroom in a baggy V-neck T-shirt and sweatpants, glasses in place.

"Hey, *bella*," he said, rolling off the bed, where he'd been lounging in boxer briefs as he liked to do every freaking night. Would it kill him to wear shorts? She couldn't take the gorgeous Italian underwear model look every night without touching. If she knew for sure that she could touch him without him touching her back in certain mushy places, she'd do it in a heartbeat.

She snorted, uncomfortable with the Italian compliment that couldn't possibly be true. She wasn't beautiful. It was a line he probably used on every woman he met. He crossed to her, sliding his hand into her hair in that drugging way he had that always made her eyes close as his large hand managed to both cradle her head and somehow communicate possession before his lips met hers in a hard, demanding kiss. She allowed herself that small pleasure. He was an amazing kisser. Before long she was moaning in the back of her throat and rubbing herself shamelessly against his hard body. But when he took her hand and pulled her toward the bed, she dug her heels in.

"I have a rash," she announced. There. No one in their right mind would want to catch a rash.

He raised a brow. "Where?"

She looked meaningfully down to her crotch.

He scowled. "You do not."

She shook her head sadly. "I think I caught something from trying on those tight jeans in Chicago."

"Lil, what is it? This right here—" he gestured to the bed "—was half the reason I agreed to the trip."

"It was?"

"Yes! Two weeks. No strings. But now we've only got eleven nights left! What's the problem?"

Her cheeks burned. This was so embarrassing. Why did he keep wanting to talk about it? She could never tell him her weird fear of not measuring up. This was just getting more and more awkward the more nights they spent not sleeping together. It wasn't supposed to be like this. It was supposed to be smooth, lusty fun. She wrung her hands together.

"What?" he barked. "Tell me."

Her eyes widened. She hadn't heard him raise his voice before. He was usually so smooth and charming like nothing ever bothered him. Even when she'd nearly gotten them killed during her truck-driving lessons, he hadn't lost his temper. But the fiery stare he was leveling her way was a little unnerving. "It's nothing."

He paced back and forth and finally stopped. "Then why do you keep turning me down?"

"I don't. I'm just..." She blew out a breath. "What's the rush? I'm sure it'll happen by Vegas. I'll have too much to drink. You'll have too much to drink. We'll crash in bed in the dark and not remember a thing in the morning." She held up a finger. "Something to look forward to!"

He studied her for a moment. "Is that what you really want?"

She lifted one shoulder up and down. She looked at her feet. "I'm a virgin." She felt like one, anyway. Being with John had been such a quick, in the dark kind of thing. She'd hardly done anything before it was over.

He was silent. She risked a look at him. His expression said concerned with a little pity thrown her way. "Really?" he asked.

"Kinda."

"Kinda?" He slammed his hands on his hips. "How're you *kinda* a virgin?"

"Fine, there's no kinda about it. I'm a twenty-five-year-old virgin!" She bit her lip and looked away. Guilt over the lie pricked at her conscience. But there was no way she could tell him the truth. That her past lover had to think of someone else just to sleep with her. That she was Godzilla in bed.

"Why don't I believe you?" he asked.

She met his eyes, knowing she was a terrible liar, and blurted, "They called me Slutty Spencer in high school."

"Fine!" he barked. "Don't tell me. We'll just wait until Vegas for your drunken night." He turned and headed past her to the bathroom.

"In the dark," she reminded him.

He stopped and slowly turned around. "That part important to you?"

She shrugged. He headed for the light switch and turned the light off. She fumbled in the dark for the switch on the other side of the room and whacked her knee on the dresser, but she did it. She turned the light on while she stood way on the other side of the room.

"I can't figure you out at all," he said.

"I'm a mystery wrapped in an enigma."

He stared at her for a long moment. "You're

something. Do you want me to get a separate room?"

Her eyes widened. It would be much more difficult to get over her nerves if she had to actually go knock on his door. "No."

He shoved both hands in his hair, and then smoothed it back. "So is our deal off? The no-strings fling?"

"Let's just wait for Vegas. Okay?"

He groaned and headed for the bathroom. He really liked to relax with a shower at the end of the day. And one in the morning too. She had to give him points for good hygiene.

CHAPTER TEN

It was seven and a half hours to Denver, and Nico considered driving straight through to Vegas. He couldn't, of course. It was another eleven hours from Denver to Vegas and it wasn't safe to skip sleep, but damn, he really needed Vegas to happen as soon as possible. For some reason, Lily wanted them to have a drunken tumble. Hell, if it helped her nerves, he'd let her have a few drinks, but he wouldn't be drunk. He wanted to remember every moment of their night together. He'd spent half the night listening to her breathe through those soft plump lips. That bow at the top drove him crazy. Those breasts that he knew would fill his hands, full and soft. They were real too, he'd seen the fake kind plenty. And all that soft kissable skin. The woman smelled like cherries all the time, it was her lipstick or shampoo or something. He didn't know. All he knew was that he wanted to lick every inch of her.

He took a shuddering breath and risked a glance over at her sitting on the passenger side of the truck. She was drifting off again to the sound of the bar exam review. He wasn't surprised. That review course could put anyone to sleep. He had to learn patience with her. Just because she'd said he was smoking hot and that she'd sleep with him didn't mean she was just going to jump in the sack. He hadn't had to go slow in so long that he was screwing it up. He was pushing her too much. With Lily a kiss didn't mean straight to bed.

He didn't wake her for lunch. Just ate one of the two granola bars he'd bought at the hotel gift shop this morning. He'd gotten into the habit of working out for an hour before Lily woke, needing to work through the tension of yet another night of being close to her, but not touching. He spent way too much time thinking about her at night. All of her different expressions, whether she was smiling or worried or, as he was starting to pick up on, her guilty, lying face. He couldn't believe the whoppers she came out with. At least she was a terrible liar. A rash from trying on jeans. Please.

He also thought a lot about the way she really got a kick out of the simple things in life, despite having grown up in a wealthy family. You just couldn't fake that enthusiasm over a giant spaghetti fork in the middle of Omaha, or those salt and pepper shakers that were tacky at best, hideous at worst. They'd spent more than three hours in that salt and pepper shaker museum, and when they came out, she was beaming and chattering away about all the "adorable" shakers she'd seen. He hoped she didn't have any plans for starting her own collection. He liked the minimalist look at home.

Wait, they weren't living together. Being on the road created a strange intimacy between them—sharing a room at night, sharing the small confines of the truck cab all day. Even if they weren't talking, he was hyperaware of her. Every breath, every sigh, every shift of her body. Her scent, cherry and fresh soap and sweet Lily. The way her cheeks colored bright pink when she was embarrassed or just excited. Her voice was sultry at times, other times more like a song. The way she twirled her silky red hair between her fingers when she was getting tired.

Oh, man, he had it bad.

He forced his mind away from Lily. He was looking forward to watching his brother Vince get shackled. Vince had once been a player with an impressive way of going from meet to sheets in a matter of an hour or two. He wondered if any of his brothers had advice for seducing a blushing virgin like Lily. He didn't actually think she was a virgin, but from the way she reacted to his moves, which were normally extremely successful, she was damn close to one. Vince would say to wait for the signal and break the touch barrier as soon as possible. But he'd done that. He touched her all the time, holding hands, arm around the shoulder, kissing. She liked the kissing. He knew she did. She was hot and moaning in his arms. He got hard. Dammit. Stop thinking about Lily!

There was nothing around for miles, just road and more road, and she was right there, all curves and softness. Maybe he could toss a blanket in the back of the flatbed and take her there. No. She wanted a soft bed. She wanted a slowie.

He couldn't go any slower. He'd die.

She sighed softly in her sleep and shifted to her side. Luke would tell him to smooth talk her. Nico wasn't great with words. He depended on a killer smile and a few well-chosen lines. Most women liked being called *bella*, beautiful in Italian. Usually he'd joke around with them a bit. Nothing he usually did worked with Lily. Sure, she liked joking around, but it never led to where he wanted it to go. She had some kind of hang-up. It wasn't him. He could feel the chemistry between them, which seemed to grow every time he kissed her. Even when she was pulling away, he sensed she wanted to go for it. She was conflicted, which made him conflicted.

That was it. Tonight he'd get to the bottom of

whatever it was that was stopping her, reassure her, and then he could stop obsessing over her.

He drove for another half hour, stealing glances at her sleeping. She looked like a sexy angel. He reconsidered his earlier decision to cut the trip short and make it back in time for Vince's bachelor party. He needed a little more time with her. What was he going to see there anyway, some stripper? All he wanted to see was Lily. Her skin was like the pale pink of a rose, soft like a petal—

Shut up. He needed to get his man card back. Since when did he get so poetic? She was making him crazy.

She sat up suddenly, pulling the headphones off. "Did I miss lunch?"

He handed her a granola bar.

"That's it?"

"That's it." They were five hours to Denver, and he couldn't wait. He had to get her naked ASAP, so he could stop being a damn swooning poet, pining at her feet.

"Are you putting me on a diet?" she asked.

"No." He knew the right answer to that one. Women were damn touchy about their weight. Besides, she didn't need to lose weight. She was perfect.

"Then why didn't you stop for lunch?"

"We really need to get to Denver. We'll have an early dinner."

She tore the wrapper off the granola bar and took a bite. A moment later, she said, "You shouldn't have let me sleep so long."

"At least now you'll be awake tonight."

"Why would I want to be awake at night?"

"There are reasons."

"Like what?" she asked in a hostile tone. "Oh. Never mind."

"Yeah."

"I could really use some tequila tonight."

"You really need alcohol to sleep with me?"

She went back to her granola bar, color in her cheeks high. He'd get to the bottom of this if it killed him. But not now. Once he was kissing her. It was a more natural time to ease her into the subject.

"No tequila," he said.

"You're not as much fun as I thought you'd be," she pouted.

The remark stung. Everyone said he was fun. He was always joking around, having a good time. Lily had made him cranky, and there was only one solution.

"I'll be more fun tonight," he said.

"Can't wait," she muttered.

He bit back what he felt like yelling. He never got

mad, never liked to fight. He and his ex had spent half their marriage yelling at each other, and he'd hated it.

"Ooh, Nico, I almost forgot. Colorado has beer can folk art. We could—"

"No."

"But it's only about—"

"We will not be stopping for *any* reason."

A moment passed in silence.

"I need the restroom," she said.

"You do not. You're trying to delay. You can hold it."

"I really can't. Stop at the next rest area. Maybe they'll have some salt and pepper shakers there!"

"You're not starting a collection, are you?"

"I'm going to send it to that museum in Traer. It's my new quest to help them be the world's largest collection. You know, instead of the second largest. Sounds a lot better, doesn't it?"

He sighed inwardly. It was a nice sentiment, but he didn't want to spend the rest of their trip stopping all over the place for salt and pepper shakers.

"Ooh, look!" she exclaimed. "That billboard says they have skydiving nearby. Let's stop."

"Skydiving? From the woman who was terrified of the Ferris wheel?"

"I was not terrified. I was brave. You said I had courage. I'm trying to face my fears. Besides, the sign said you go in tandem with an instructor."

"So that cancels out free-falling thousands of feet?"

"Of course! The instructor doesn't want to die. They wouldn't take the job if it was dangerous."

"We're *not* going skydiving."

"Have you ever been?"

"No." His brother Jared had many times. He was the adrenaline junkie, not Nico.

"C'mon, it'll be fun. And I'll never be scared of heights again after that. It's like my Mount Everest."

He let out a long-suffering sigh. "Lil."

"Please, Nico. After this trip, I'll be cramming for the bar exam and then I'll be chained to a desk and I'll never have any fun again."

He considered that. He wanted her to have good memories of their trip. The best two-week vacation/fling of her life. All because of him.

"It is something you'd never forget," he said.

"Absolutely!"

"Are you sure?"

"I'm sure."

"Okay, we'll go skydiving."

"Woo-hoo!" She beamed at him and squeezed his bicep, which made him feel all gooey inside.

Hell, he'd give her anything she wanted.

Anything but his heart.

~ ~ ~

Lily sat through a forty-five-minute training video and detailed instructions from the crew that ran the skydiving company with something approaching dread. What did it say about her that she'd rather fling herself out of an airplane than rush to get naked in a hotel room with the sexiest man on the planet?

Nico seemed tense, so she kept giving him the thumbs-up sign with a smile. He returned the smile with something approaching a grimace. That was fine if he was nervous about skydiving too. This experience would bond them together. She'd never forget the time she leaped to her death to avoid sex.

They were the only two jumping this afternoon, so that made the experience even more intense. The plan was, they would be strapped in front of their instructor for a tandem jump. The instructor would pull the chute. All they had to do was keep their hands out of the way by hanging onto the straps of their harness while the instructor positioned them at the plane's opening and pushed off. Sounded simple enough. Just close your eyes and fall.

Once their harnesses and safety goggles were on, they walked over to the tiny prop plane with the pilot and the two tandem instructors they'd be jumping with. She slowed her steps.

Nico's arm dropped over her shoulders. "Having second thoughts?"

She smiled up at him. "Nope."

"The fee is nonrefundable," the instructor, Alex, said with a laugh. Alex was a thin, wiry man with a light of adventure in his blue eyes. She was glad he was her partner because Mike, the other instructor, was a beefy guy with a beard that she did *not* want to fall on top of her.

Lily laughed heartily along with Alex. It paid to stay on the good side of the man you were strapped to when jumping out of a plane.

"You ready to celebrate life?" Mike asked in his gung-ho tone.

"Sure," Nico said.

"Absolutely!" Lily exclaimed, matching Mike's enthusiasm.

"Right on," Mike said, giving her a high five. "You're gonna love it." Mike turned to Nico. "Heaviest one goes first to save on fuel, so that's us. You ready, man?"

Nico inclined his head. "Ready as I'll ever be."

"That's the spirit," Mike said, slapping Nico on the shoulder.

They piled into the tiny plane, which was noisy from the propellers, and hot. She and Nico were strapped in place in front of Alex and Mike respectively. The plane raced down the runway, shaking with the power of the wind, and Lily knew a moment of pure terror. What was she doing? How was this facing her fears? Her real fear was on the ground, dealing with her own body issues and ex-fiancé hang-ups. What would this prove?

And then they were airborne. She closed her eyes and tried to breathe normally. Finally the plane leveled out, and she opened her eyes to find Nico staring at her. His gaze was intense. She wanted to ask him what he was thinking, but it was noisy, and they were strapped to two strange men who didn't need to hear that conversation.

Their gazes locked. She couldn't tear herself away. Something welled up in her, some strong emotion. She wasn't sure what it was or where it had come from, him or her, but it was there, this palpable connection, a thousand feet in the air.

Before she knew it, Mike was signaling it was time. He opened the small hatch door on the side of the plane. Lily caught a glimpse of open sky and moved from worry to panic about what they were about to do.

"You pumped?" Mike hollered to Nico strapped to his front.

"Yeah," Nico said. He glanced longingly over Mike's shoulder at her, and then Mike maneuvered them to the opening of the plane.

Omigod. It was really happening. She peeked out

the window. They were above some clouds, but she could make out the flat, square farmland of Nebraska, patches of yellow and green laid out below them. She suddenly felt sick.

Then Nico and Mike were gone. Her heart raced. She heard nothing at first but the wind. For a heartbreaking moment, she feared she'd lost Nico forever before she ever had a chance to experience the wonder that was her Italian underwear model.

She let out a primal scream. "Nico!" She turned to Alex in a sweaty, panicky state and said over her shoulder, "Come on. Let's go. We have to go now."

"Not yet. They need time to land."

She couldn't lose Nico. She'd just found him. She tried to get up, but Alex was too heavy on her back.

"Hang on there," Alex said. "It'll be our turn soon."

Moments ticked by while Lily's heart raced. She felt like running and screaming and crying all at the same time as she sat helplessly waiting. Finally, Alex pushed up from the seat.

"Ready?" he asked.

"Yes!"

They maneuvered to the plane's opening. The wind whipped at her face and there was nothing but sky as Alex grabbed a hold of the grip on the side of the plane and placed his foot on the small ledge.

Just as she felt him tense to push off, she screamed, "I changed my—"

Terror stole her voice as they hurtled toward the earth. Spinning, more terror, and then a jerk as the chute opened. Her heart slowed as another chute opened, and they were gliding.

She did it! She faced her fear! She'd never be afraid of heights again.

And then she passed out.

~ ~ ~

Nico had a real moment of terror up there in that plane and not because he was about to leap to his death with a two-hundred-pound bearded man on his back. It was because all he could think about in the moments before his death was that he was glad Lily was the last thing he'd see on earth. In that long moment gazing into her eyes, he felt something very real and terrifyingly tender lodge in the vicinity of his locked heart, nudging to be let in.

And then, thankfully, Mike was maneuvering them toward the hatch, and the moment was broken as he turned from her. There was no room for that kind of uncomfortable, tender feeling with a two-week, no-strings fling.

What followed next was a quick vision of a cloud whipping by, Mike pushing off, and sixty seconds of horrifying free fall where he unexpectedly barfed all over his instructor. The wind caught it and flung it back at Mike, who complained loudly. Some had gotten on the side of Nico's face too, but that was the least of his problems. They were spinning, flipping upside down, and that chute was not opening.

Then he jerked back as Mike finally did open it, and their descent slowed. A few moments later another chute opened, and they were gliding. The view was spectacular, but his brain and body were still trying to process the fact that he was floating in the air thousands of feet above the ground. He felt light-headed as the wind whipped at him. But it would all be worth it for Lily. She'd face her fear here, and then tonight, high on this adrenaline rush, she'd get over her nerves with him.

They glided to a smooth landing, and Mike unstrapped him. Nico had never felt so happy to have his feet touch the ground. Not even after those horrible driving lessons where Lily almost got them killed. He was shaky, and his legs felt like jelly. He turned and looked at Mike, who was taking off his goggles with some barf on them.

"Sorry about that," Nico said. "I didn't even feel it coming. It just happened."

"Don't worry, dude. Happens all the time with first-timers. At least you didn't pass out. I'll go grab some paper towels."

Mike returned from the hangar with paper towels and a couple of bottled waters. Nico wet the towel and cleaned the side of his face, then he swished the water around his mouth, spitting it out.

He looked up at the plane slowly circling high above them. He'd thought Lily would've jumped by now.

Mike must've thought so too. "Damn, your girlfriend's taking a long time. Hope everything's okay up there."

Nico froze. He wondered if she was terrified right now. He wished he could make it easier for her. And then someone appeared at the plane's opening. He caught a glimpse of red hair and his heart caught in his throat as she leaped with Alex.

He paced back and forth, waiting for Lily to land on the ground again safe and sound. As she came into view, on a slow glide, she looked weird. Eyes closed, mouth slack, just kind of hanging there. Oh, shit. She was unconscious.

Alex landed gently and eased to his back, so Lily was flat on her back on top of him. "Get her off me. She passed out."

Mike lumbered over and unstrapped Lily from Alex and laid her on the ground. He slapped her cheek rapidly. "Wake up."

Nico shoved him out of the way and pressed the cool water bottle to her forehead. "Lil, hey. Open your eyes. You did it."

She didn't respond. He carefully removed her goggles. "Come on, baby. Wake up."

"Throw some water on her," Alex said.

"Don't," Nico snapped. He bent down toward her ear, brushing her hair back. "Wake up. They got those salt and pepper shakers you like. Airplanes. Fucking adorable."

Her eyelids fluttered and those electric blues landed on him. "Nico. You're alive."

He pulled her up and held her tight. "Yeah. Piece of cake."

She buried her head in his chest. "I thought I'd lost you."

That uncomfortable feeling was back, an ache in his chest. He was not ready to deal with that. "Can you walk?"

"I saw nothing but sky, and then you were gone! I panicked. I thought you were about to die—"

"I *was* about to die."

She laughed then, a big, semi-hysterical, but happy laugh. A smile tugged at his lips even though this whole thing had been a damn miserable experience. He'd barfed, for crying out loud. She passed out. How was that fun?

She hugged him tight again.

"Come on, you two lovebirds," Alex said. "We've got a debriefing. And then you can get those salt and pepper shakers at the gift shop."

Lily's eyes widened. "They really have those?"

He pulled her to her feet and wrapped an arm around her shoulders. "Let's go."

They headed back to the hangar with the crew. Lily made small talk with the men while Nico pondered what had gotten into him. Why had he agreed to skydive? Just because she smiled when he gave her what she wanted? That was pathetic. And not the way he wanted things to go between them. He had to be more firm with her. Who knew what she'd try to talk him into next?

Once they got back in the truck and on the road, Lily glanced sideways at him. "Think you'll ever do it again?"

"Hell no." He jabbed a finger at her. "And that was our absolute last stop. We're heading straight to Denver after this. No stopping for any reason. Do I make myself clear?"

She saluted. "Sir, yes, sir!"

~ ~ ~

Several hours later, after a stop for dinner, the restroom, and more salt and pepper shakers in the hotel gift shop, Nico finally got Lily into the hotel room. It was nearly ten o'clock, much later than he'd planned, but after a quick shower and brushing his teeth, he had her right where he wanted her. In his arms. He kissed her for a really, really long time, until her lips were swollen from his kisses, and she was mewling in the back of her throat and writhing restlessly against him. And then, finally, at long last, he led her to the bed.

She pulled away.

Those sweatpants of hers shifted dangerously low. *Drop*, he thought desperately, *please drop*. He was nearly out of patience, nearly out of sweet talk. He had to make this happen before he went fucking insane.

"Lil," he said with as much gentle restraint as possible, "you conquered your fears today. You were a total badass jumping from that plane. Why're you afraid of me?"

She snorted. "I'm not afraid of you." One corner of her mouth lifted. "You really think I'm a badass?"

"Yes."

She smiled. "You are too."

"I know. Take off your clothes."

She flushed bright pink. "Nico."

"What's the problem?" he barked, completely out of patience.

She sighed, looked all around the room and finally

settled her hands on her hips belligerently, meeting his gaze with those electric blue eyes of hers. He felt the jolt like he always did when their eyes met. "I'm not as hot as you, okay?" she said. "It's intimidating."

He smiled. This was no problem at all. "You're very hot." He stepped closer, and she put up a hand.

"I have a pooch."

His brows scrunched together in confusion. "What's a pooch?"

"You know, a tummy."

He smiled. "I like curves. I like softness."

"Thank you, goodnight."

"You don't believe me."

"Be serious."

He leaned closer. "How's this for serious? Three nights of blue balls because of you. An entire week before that when I tried to teach you to drive the truck."

"Really?"

He threw his hands up. "Yeah, really!"

She went to his side and stroked his arm. "That's the nicest thing anyone has ever said to me."

"I jerk off every night in the shower thinking of that mouth," he admitted.

She leaned against his side. "You are so sweet."

He grunted. "Let me see your pooch."

"Nico."

"Come on, I'm dying here. I can't take ten more nights of blue balls."

She just stood there.

He pulled rank. "I skydived for you. That was not my idea of fun. I almost *died*."

She frowned. "You did not almost die. You just felt like you were dying."

"Stop stalling."

She closed her eyes and lifted her T-shirt. Her belly was round and cute. He looked up to her face, where her eyes were shut tight. His chest ached at the way she bared herself to him. The way she faced her fear of rejection head-on even though it was difficult for her. Just like on the Ferris wheel when she faced her fear of heights. The way she faced her fear of heights again today, completely conquering it.

He dropped to his knees in front of her, kissed her soft belly, and inhaled her sweet, fresh scent. And that was it.

He was done for.

CHAPTER ELEVEN

"Nico," Lily said hesitantly, "what're you doing?" He was still on his knees, hugging her, his stubbled cheek pressed against the sensitive skin of her stomach.

He looked up at her with what could only be described as adoration in his deep brown eyes. Her heart kicked up. "I love your pooch," he said.

And she believed him.

He rose to his feet in one fluid motion, wrapped his arms around her, and kissed her. And this time she kissed him back with all the passion she felt every time he kissed her, no holding back, no fear of him touching her and being disappointed. It was glorious. And then he lifted her and carried her to the bed, and she nearly swooned at the gesture. He joined her a moment later, lying on his side, kissing her, stroking her cheek and jaw, taking his time with her. She fell with a stuttering, heart-dropping crash as she finally let herself enjoy what he offered. She ran her hands all over him, across his broad shoulders, his biceps, his amazing chest. He was kissing her neck now, and she tilted her head to let him, her lips parting on a sigh.

He pushed up her T-shirt, and she lifted slightly to help him take it off. She lay back down as he took her in. A sliver of doubt kicked in as he gazed at her breasts and lower to her belly for long moments before reaching out to touch. His warm hand cupped her breast, his thumb stroking over her nipple, and she arched into his hand, needing more. His mouth soon followed as he kissed all along the sensitive underside, round and round, before closing in on the rigid peak and sucking hard. Heat flooded her, and she moaned. He moved to the other breast, again with the slow kisses and hard sucking that made sensation shoot through her.

Then he stopped and met her eyes for a long moment. She couldn't tell what he was thinking, good or bad. She panicked.

"What're you thinking about?" she asked, very worried that it was some supermodel pinup he had to picture to be with her. She shut her eyes tight. This wasn't her ex. Still, the fear gripped her.

He kissed her closed eyelids, kissed her cheek, and leaned down to whisper the extremely dirty thing he wanted to do to her. Her eyes flew open. Her. He wanted her. A rush of affection and gratitude filled her heart. She wrapped her arms around him. "Really?"

His lips brushed across hers before he sucked her lower lip into his mouth. He released her and met her eyes. "Hell yeah. I want you so bad, Lil." Then he slid down her baggy sweatpants and her plain white panties and the next thing she knew he was between her legs, kissing, licking, sucking, and she exploded only a few minutes later from the shocking intimacy and incredible feeling.

He sat back and stared at her. "I can't believe you came so quick. I was just getting started."

She stretched languorously, still warm and liquid, all of her muscles completely relaxed. "Mmm."

Next thing she knew, Nico was naked and pressing his whole body against hers. She wrapped her arms and legs around all that delicious man. He stroked her hair back from her face and slowly traced her lips with his tongue. "Lil?"

She opened her eyes. He was so wonderful. She was so lucky. "Yes?"

"Was that your first orgasm?"

"N-no," she stuttered out, her cheeks burning. She did not want to talk about this after that. She'd had plenty of orgasms. Just not with another person involved. She thought horrible thoughts about her ex for always making her feel less than and never making the kind of effort Nico did. She grabbed his ass. "Let's do it."

But he didn't make any movement in that direction. Instead he started kissing her all over again, from her cheeks to her throat, down to her breasts, her belly, her inner thighs, and shockingly he kept going, kissing her legs, all the way down to her toes. She'd never felt so lit up inside. "Don't you want to—"

"Not done yet," he said in a hoarse voice before he rolled her over onto her belly and started massaging her legs, starting with her calves. His mouth followed the path of his hands up her legs. It was like a massage only heightened by the fact that the most gorgeous man in the world was doing it. Now his hands were on her ass and she squirmed, which made him linger, massaging and cupping her until he spread her legs wide. His hand slid between her legs, making her jolt.

"I'm a lucky man," he murmured. She had no idea what he meant by that, but she didn't have any time to figure it out because he was kissing and licking the dip in her lower back and then he was moving up her back, across her shoulders, and she was a melted, sparking puddle of need. He slid her hair to the side and kissed the nape of her neck, his teeth scraping and then biting down gently. Electric frissons of sensation shot down her spine. She wanted him. Wanted this.

"Nico," she moaned. "Please."

"Tell me what you're into," he growled in her ear,

his heat warming her back.

She was nearly vibrating with need. She had no idea, no experience to draw from. "I'm into whatever you're into."

He groaned and rolled her to her back. She grabbed him, pulling him in for a frantic kiss, feeling like she was on the edge of something marvelous. She rocked her pelvis against him, his thick erection pressing into her belly.

"I promised you slow," he said, his voice rough and gravelly.

"I need more. Please."

He kissed her, hot and deep, and she was lost, there was nothing but Nico's mouth claiming hers. His hand slid between her legs, and she arched into him, moaning like a crazed sex-deprived woman. Which she totally was.

"Easy," he said, before sliding lower and slipping his fingers inside her. "Geez, you're tight."

She couldn't speak, could only move restlessly, wanting more.

"Lil, look at me."

She opened her eyes with great effort.

"You have to tell me if this is your first time."

She shook her head. "It's not. I'm sorry I'm so tight. It's been a while."

His fingers were back, sliding in and out of her,

stretching her. "How long?" His voice was raspy.

"Two years. Please don't make me wait any longer."

He groaned and then his mouth slammed into hers, a thorough claiming that had her almost dizzy with want. Oh, this was what she'd been missing all her life. This passion. His fingers slid out of her and then slid up and down her, and she writhed under him before he pressed firmly in the spot where she needed him most, and she exploded again. His forehead dropped to hers, his breath coming hard. "I've never seen anything like it."

"Is that good or bad?"

He chuckled and kissed her gently. "That's very good," he said against her mouth.

"Now?" she asked.

"Just a minute, you horny little thing." He went to his suitcase to get a condom, she figured. She felt giddy. No one had ever called her horny or little. And then he was back, settling between her legs, and she wrapped her arms and legs around him. He propped himself on his forearms and gazed down at her, his eyes dark and heated. "I'm so glad you picked me. You're incredible."

She could scarcely believe the words, but they shot right through her heart, settling there in a strange uncomfortable way. She kissed him and then he was sliding inside very, very slowly and her body ached as she strained to accept him.

He stopped and looked at her. Sweat beaded on his forehead. She wiped it away and ran her fingers through his soft dark brown hair. "It's okay," she said. "You don't have to go slow."

"I do." He slid further in, and she ached even more. Two years was a long time not to be with a man, and he was so thick.

"Are you almost in?" she asked in a strained voice.

He dropped his head and kissed her shoulder. "No."

She let out a shuddering breath. And then he lifted off her slightly so his hand could slide down and stroke her where she was coming to crave his touch, and that so distracted her from the ache that she completely relaxed, and he slid further in. She gasped and then his magical fingers were back, stroking her up and down lazily, like he had all night, and the orgasm snuck up on her, making her cry out, her hips lifting of their own accord, and then he was fully within her. And now she was the one sweating.

"You're so beautiful," he said as he started to move slowly in and out, and the words combined with the easy strokes made her relax a bit more as she tried not to think about the intense stretching that heated her and made her ache at the same time.

"You're so wonderful," she said.

"Lil." He slid his fingers between them once more and she lifted up, eager for his touch, and unexpectedly took him deeper. They both groaned. "One more time," he told her, his fingers stroking quickly even as he pumped slow and deep. It was too much, the combination of electric strokes and deep aches filling her. She went off like a rocket, clenching around him.

And then he thrust hard, over and over, taking what he needed, and she clung to him until he let go with a hoarse sound that might've been her name. Her arms and legs dropped to her sides, her legs quivering from the tight hold she'd had on him.

A few moments later, he took care of the condom and pulled her close in his arms, placing a kiss on her hair. Her ex never held her after. She snuggled closer, resting her head on his chest, listening to the solid thump of his heartbeat.

She couldn't imagine saying goodbye to him in ten days. Why had she acted so casual about going their separate ways? Would he feel the same? She didn't want to be clingy. She had abandonment issues, she well knew, on account of what waited for her in Vegas.

She pushed that uncomfortable thought aside. Her body still felt electrified. Four orgasms in one night! She was a very lucky woman.

CHAPTER TWELVE

Nico was freaking out as he set out on the eleven-hour drive to Vegas. He could admit it. To himself, not Lily. Because he was feeling all gooey and tender toward the woman he was supposed to say goodbye to in nine short days. She would start her new lawyer life in the city; he'd go back to being a grease monkey in Eastman. She was way out of his league, and he couldn't afford to screw things up with her father. Not to mention he was never getting married again.

Whoa. Where had that thought come from? He pressed the accelerator even harder. It must be because they were going to Vegas. Lots of people got married there. He was never—

"Nico?" Her sweet voice cut through his panic, and he answered in a tender tone because she'd trusted him last night.

"Yes?" He glanced over at her. The headphones were askew on her head, her red hair was all windblown, her lips plump and pink. She had whisker burn on the side of her neck. He wanted her so freaking bad.

"Maybe we should slow down a bit," she said.

Relief coursed through him. She must be feeling it too, this headlong crash into dangerous territory. Love territory.

"I was thinking the same thing," he said.

A beat passed in silence while he pondered how to pull up at this point. Because he felt like there weren't any brakes on this thing between them.

"You're still not slowing down," she said. "You're going one hundred miles per hour."

He glanced at the speedometer. Shit. He eased off the gas. "Sorry."

"Everything okay?" she asked, almost shyly.

"Fine." He didn't want to hurt her feelings with his panicky thoughts. Not after the way she offered herself again this morning, even as she admitted upon questioning that she was sore. He'd gone down on her instead, and she went off in two minutes flat. Freaking amazingly responsive. He wondered if it was just him or if she was like that with all of her lovers. Though he knew there couldn't have been many.

"Hey, Lil, not that it matters, but how many people have you slept with?"

"How many have you slept with?"

"I dunno. Maybe forty?"

"Forty!" she screeched. It was probably more. He didn't keep track anymore, but he'd been hooking up since he was sixteen. He'd been faithful for the year he'd been married, they'd only dated three months before that, so that had slowed him down.

"Don't worry," he said. "I always use protection. I get tested regularly. I'm clean."

A long silence.

"Are you upset?" he asked.

She said something so softly that he couldn't make out what she said.

"What?" he asked.

"I said two. Including you. I've slept with two men."

That explained a helluva lot. But she enjoyed it so much he couldn't imagine why she'd deprived herself for so many years.

He reached over and squeezed her hand. "Can I ask why? Were you with that one guy for a long time?"

"We were together for a year."

"Oh. Then why?"

Silence. He tensed. What had that one guy done to her? He'd kill him.

"Lil, you can tell me anything. I won't tell a soul." Then I'll kill him.

She let out a sigh. "The reason why I haven't slept

with a lot of men is because a lot of men haven't wanted to sleep with me."

"What do you mean?"

"I mean I don't get asked out a lot. I'm not, you know, the ideal woman in terms of, um, looks."

"You've got to be kidding me. You're gorgeous, sexy." He gestured up and down her body. "Look at all those curves. You're like a redheaded Marilyn Monroe. Smart—"

"Really? You think I look like Marilyn Monroe?"

"Better."

"Omigod, I'm going to cry."

He looked at her with alarm. "Don't cry. It's a compliment."

"I know." Her voice sounded choked with emotion. "You're something, Nico. Really. Thank you."

He shrugged. He'd only pointed out the facts. That one guy must've done a number on her to make her think she wasn't sexy. She was sexy in anything she wore and anything she did. Even now, in just a simple T-shirt and shorts, Sex Lollipop. He didn't know where that thought had come from, but that got him thinking about that mouth again on him, and he wasn't going to make it to Vegas with that erotic vision stuck in his head. They still had ten more hours to go. He forced his thoughts to marriage, the ultimate doomsday scenario that always put him in a cold sweat.

Only this time, it didn't work.

~ ~ ~

By the time they got to Vegas around ten at night, Lily was freaking out. Not over Nico. He was impossibly wonderful. She still couldn't quite believe he was into her. No, the problem was what she knew she had to do in Vegas. Which was why she promptly decided to get drunk.

They checked into the Paris Las Vegas hotel because Lily loved the kitschy Eiffel Tower in front. Nico crashed on one of the two queen-sized beds, kicking off his shoes and stretching out. He must've been exhausted after that long drive, but she wasn't.

"C'mere," he said in a sultry, seductive voice that pulled at her.

"I'm not tired."

"Don't make me get up," he said on a near groan.

"I'm going to go gamble and get drunk," she said, grabbing her purse.

He leaped out of bed. "I'm coming with you."

He couldn't come with her. Then he'd meet the one person she didn't want him to meet.

"You just relax," she said. "I plan on staying out all night, so you might not want to come."

He crossed his arms. "So I'm just supposed to let a young, beautiful, sexy woman loose on this town all drunk? Fuck that."

She melted. He was just so charming. Really good with the sweet words.

She shrugged. "Suit yourself."

He eyed her as he put his shoes back on. "I will."

Lily rode the elevator downstairs with Nico, who kept staring at her with a hot look in his eyes. But she couldn't be distracted from her mission. When they got to the casino, she went straight to the bar and ordered tequila. The one drink she knew would do the job fast. Nico got a beer.

She downed the shot and sucked on a lime. Nico groaned and wrapped an arm around her shoulders, pulling her close and nuzzling into the side of her neck. She sighed, already feeling looser.

"The way you suck that lime, Lil." He whispered in her ear what it made him think of, which made her go hot all over. That was one move she knew how to do, and what she wouldn't give to see the very experienced Nico lose control, completely at her mercy.

He flashed a smile that said he knew she was into it too. "You want to go upstairs? Just for twenty minutes or so?"

"Yeah, I wish." She needed more liquid courage for

her mission. If she took the easy way out and went to bed with Nico, she'd never want to leave the hotel room.

He wrapped his arms around her, pulling her off the bar stool to stand between his legs. "Don't wish," he crooned in her ear. "Let's make that dream come true. If you only knew—"

She laughed and pushed at his chest. "I didn't gamble yet. I've got two hundred dollars in my pocket looking to multiply." She slipped away, headed over to the roulette table and watched the pretty wheel spin round and round.

"That is a sure loser," Nico said, grabbing her by the hips and pulling her in front of him. She could feel why as he pressed hard against her hip. "Why don't you try blackjack? At least there's a little skill involved. This game is rigged to lose."

"Pshaw," she said. They stood together, watching the game. When the casino guy called for bets again, she put all her money on red three.

Nico appeared at her side and shook his head. "I hope you have more cash."

"Nope. This is it, but I think I'm going to win big."

"I hate to break it to you—"

"Red three," the casino guy said.

Lily screamed and started jumping up and down.

"That's me!" She giggled madly and took her winnings. She'd won twelve thousand dollars.

"I can't believe it," Nico said.

"Drinks on me all night," she said airily.

"I don't want anything. Maybe we should put that money upstairs in the safe."

Lily scowled. "I need it with me to have fun."

He shook his head. Lily collected her winnings at the casino cage in the form of a ten-thousand-dollar check and two thousand dollars in cash. She drank more tequila and wasted many quarters in slots while Nico stood nearby like a soldier, guarding her. Finally it was midnight, she was drunk, and she was ready for what she had to do.

"C'mon," she told Nico, pulling at his arm. "We're going to see a show."

"A show?" he echoed.

"Yeah, this is Vegas, showgirls, feathers, the works." She lifted her arms over her head and did a little hip wiggle to demonstrate.

His brows scrunched together as they often did with her. "You want to watch showgirls? I thought that was just for men."

She stopped and rolled her eyes. "It's entertainment."

He held up his palms. "Okay, but I'm holding that check."

"It's perfectly safe in my purse."

"Everyone in the casino heard you screaming about your win. I don't want someone trying something with you."

She pouted. He kissed her, sucking her lower lip into his mouth. When he released her, he was holding her purse.

"Nico!"

"I'll give it back to you when we get back to the room. I just want you to be safe."

She opened her purse and handed the check to him. He glanced around and stuck it in his wallet before sliding it into his pocket. "Thank you."

"Since when did you get so bossy?" she complained.

"Since you drank three tequilas and won—" he lowered his voice "—a buttload of money."

She giggled. "The check has my name on it, you know."

"I'm sure someone could forge your signature."

"Ha!" She turned and headed to the exit, weaving in and out of all the shiny slot machines. Nico gripped her elbow suddenly and steered her in the opposite direction to the exit.

Once they were outside, she looked up and down the strip, trying to get her bearings. She pointed right. "This way!"

"Are you sure?"

"I'm sure." She pulled him along, way down the strip and to a side street to a seedy-looking club that she'd been to before, The Pink Navel. "This is it."

"Is this a strip bar?"

"No, they don't strip. They dance." She paid the cover fee, and they went into the dark, dingy room with the stage at the other end. This was the entire purpose of her trip. She didn't care about her grandfather's things, who she'd never met, didn't care about the Mustang, what she cared about more than anything was the knowledge housed in the brain of one forty-three-year-old showgirl.

CHAPTER THIRTEEN

Nico was confused. Lily was acting so strangely. For most of this trip, she'd been bubbly and enthusiastic about visiting weird stuff like rubber stamps, salt and pepper shakers, and giant forks, yet now that they were in Vegas, where most people would be having a good time, she was grimly working her way toward complete drunkenness and losing all her money. And this seedy dive was not what he ever pictured someone classy like Lily being interested in. The music started, a real old-school striptease type of song, and a dozen women filed on stage in barely there costumes made up of feathers and strategically placed sequins. Each woman wore her hair up, fake smile plastered on, their heads held high to hold up an elaborate plume of pink feathers.

It didn't do much for him, but Lily was entranced. She studied each woman, carefully watching their movements, before she fixated on the woman on the end.

He studied the woman too. She had red hair. And then he suddenly realized why Lily had been acting so strange. This must be her sister. They looked similar except the other woman looked hard and tough, her body sculpted with toned muscles.

"Is that your sister?" he asked.

Lily startled and downed her tequila. "No. Why would you say that?"

"She looks like you."

Lily kept staring at the woman, swallowing visibly.

"You know her?" he asked.

"Shh. Can you get me another drink?"

"No."

"Please? I'll do that thing you wanted."

"You're seriously bribing me with a blowjob for another drink?"

She finally tore her gaze from the woman and leaned into him, her voice a throaty purr. "I'm seriously bribing you with a blowjob. Interested?"

His cock was at full attention, so yeah. He gave her a curt nod and headed for the bar in the back to get the drink. While he waited in line, he thought again about the woman that Lily was so fascinated by. Then it hit him. If it wasn't her sister, maybe it was her mother. He knew she had a stepmom back home.

He returned to her side and handed her the drink.

Lily did the shot, sucking on the lime. She kissed him aggressively, giving him tongue, and though he knew her aggression was just because she was drunk, he couldn't help but return it.

"Thank you," she slurred, her eyes hazy with alcohol and lust. It was a good thing he was with her, that was for sure.

"When was the last time you saw your mom?" he asked.

She stiffened; then she gave him a small smile. "My mom likes fancy teas and lunch dates. When she can fit me in. Aren't I lucky?"

His brows drew together. Fancy teas didn't exactly sound like a Vegas showgirl. Maybe he'd been way off base.

They stayed for an hour and a half more, and Nico made sure Lily didn't have any more shots. Five was plenty for the night as evidenced by the frequent dirty dancing she did against his leg despite the fact that no one in the audience was dancing. He'd been forced to stand for the dirty dancing when she nearly knocked his chair over while attempting a lap dance. The show finally finished.

"Time to face the music," Lily sang before rushing the stage.

"Wait up," he called.

A security guard stopped her before she could get

on stage.

"Taylor!" Lily called, jumping up and down and waving. "Taylor!"

The red-haired woman turned. "Lily? What're you doing here?" She waved the security guard off and Lily bounded on stage.

"Can we talk?" Lily asked loudly.

Nico turned to the guard. "I'm with her." He crossed to Lily's side.

"Hello, handsome," the woman purred at him.

"Mom, this is my boyfriend Nico," Lily said, throwing her arm around him.

"I told you not to call me that," her mom said, looking around to make sure no one had overheard. "I'm barely hanging onto my job as it is. Come on to the girls' dressing room so I can change."

Nico tried to imagine the dignified George Spencer married to this woman and couldn't. One look at Lily next to her mom and the resemblances were astonishingly clear—the hair, the electric blue eyes, the fair skin, even the plump lips with the bow at the top. Though her mom wasn't as tall.

"Aren't the other women in there changing?" Nico asked.

"They don't mind being watched," her mom said before sashaying off, all feathers and sequins, and no love at all. His confusion over Lily's strange antics tonight vanished. He'd been lucky enough to have a kind, loving mom, who, unfortunately, died, but then he'd been extra lucky to have a kind, loving stepmom a few years later. Lily had definitely gotten the short end of the stick.

~ ~ ~

Lily was drunk, but not drunk enough to be numb. Seeing her biological mom always did a number on her. The mom who took her to fancy teas was her stepmom, the only mom she'd ever known until she was eighteen and her dad finally told her the truth about her mom. It explained a helluva lot. Why she was forever disappointing her dad, for one thing. Why her stepmom had always been so cool and distant with her. She was the result of an affair that her stepmom put up with only because of her dad's money. Lily was the living proof that her dad had strayed. Lily had persevered with her stepmom, Mona, because Mona was home a lot more than her dad. Mona had fit her in when it was convenient. Now her stepmom preferred to stay at their summer home in Newport, Rhode Island, year round.

The dressing room was full of scantily clad beautiful women, including her mom, who was now pulling on a halter top with no bra and not bothering to turn her back for privacy. It wouldn't have mattered. The room was wall-to-wall mirror. The harshness of the environment with its glaring exposed light bulbs surrounding the mirrors, the counter strewn with makeup and cigarette butts, the dirty linoleum floor, and, most of all, the reality of her mom, was sobering Lily up fast. She'd lost the giddy feeling from the tequila and instead felt extraordinarily tired.

She'd pulled Nico in with her, needing backup. She glanced over to find him staring at a point on the far wall away from the women. She could've hugged him for that. So she did, wrapping her arms around his waist.

He wrapped his arms around her in a warm embrace. She wished she could just stay like that, safe in his arms, but she had something important to ask her mom, and it couldn't wait.

She pulled away and turned to her mom. "Taylor, can we go someplace more private?"

Her mom pulled on some leggings and slipped her feet into high-heeled sandals. "Yeah, let's go. I need a smoke." She grabbed her purse. "Follow me."

They followed her out past the half-naked women, who took the time to give Nico an appraising up-and-down look, to the sidewalk. It was dark and the garish lights from the front of the club didn't quite reach them. There was only one light shining down from the side of the building. Her mom stood under the light and lit up her cigarette. "Smoke?" She offered the pack to them both, and they declined.

"To what do I owe this visit?" her mom said, letting the smoke leak out sideways from her mouth.

"I'll wait over there," Nico said, pointing a distance away in front of the club.

Lily grabbed his hand. "Stay."

He stayed.

"How are you, Mom?" Lily asked.

"Taylor. Call me Taylor."

Nico squeezed her hand.

"Taylor," Lily said.

Her mom gave her a small fake smile and took a long drag on her cigarette. "Fine. How nice of you to visit." There was no enthusiasm in her voice. Only a flat, jaded tone.

Lily took a deep breath. "Last time we spoke you mentioned you had another daughter. Where is she? How do I contact her?" Her mom had been drunk on their last phone call or she never would've let that slip.

"You a lawyer now?" her mom asked.

"Yes, I graduated. As soon as I pass the bar exam, it'll be official."

Her mom narrowed her eyes and took another long drag. "Big money now, huh? I'm proud of you, Lily. You turned out just like your dad wanted you to be."

Hardly, Lily thought. Her stepmom couldn't have kids and what her dad wanted most of all was a son to carry on the Spencer name. Taylor had been her father's mistress. She'd lied about her age, telling Lily's dad she was twenty-three when she'd only been eighteen, and had purposely gotten pregnant, hoping her dad would leave his wife for her. She'd planned to show up, hugely pregnant with the heir he'd always wanted, and win her place in the wealthy Spencer family. It turned out the ultrasound technician had incorrectly identified Lily as a boy. But that disappointment wasn't apparent until she was born. Taylor handed her over as a newborn to Lily's dad with no explanation other than a deal was a deal.

Because Lily was part of a contract between her parents. A result of Taylor's plan gone awry. Her dad had unexpectedly stopped by Taylor's condo (that he'd paid for) in Vegas while playing at a charity golf tournament. He'd been surprised to find his mistress six months pregnant, but he wouldn't marry her. Taylor threatened to give the baby boy, the Spencer heir, up for adoption. Her dad wanted his heir and got everything down in writing. He would raise the child with his wife, and Taylor would be compensated for her part in carrying on the Spencer dynasty to the tune of twenty grand a year until the heir was eighteen. And no contact between mother and son.

Taylor could've gotten a lot more money out of it. Her dad could've afforded it, but to Taylor, who'd been living in poverty before she met Lily's dad, the deal had been extraordinary. She'd agreed and had seemed content with her decision until Lily reached eighteen and the money dried up. Taylor wanted contact with her long-lost child, which was the only reason her dad ever told her about her mom. Taylor had right away started milking Lily for money instead. But Lily didn't care. Her mom was the key to understanding her whole screwed-up existence, and she'd gotten the full story piecemeal straight from her mom's mouth over the years. Her dad refused to speak of it, like it was all beneath him. But now there was another piece to the story, a sister, and Lily wanted that relationship more than anything in the world.

Nico's sharp voice cut through her memories. "You know what, Taylor? She turned out great."

Her mom smirked at Nico. He stiffened.

"I've never asked for anything from you," Lily said. "I just want to meet my sister. I didn't even know I had one until our last conversation."

"I don't remember saying that," her mom said. "I was drunk. Probably rambling on about a lot of things that weren't true."

"This was very specific. You said she was mad at

you for giving her up. That she didn't understand like I did. Taylor, please, a name, a phone number, anything."

Her mom stubbed out her cigarette with her sandal, grinding it into the sidewalk. "What's it worth to you?"

"You want her to pay to meet her own sister?" Nico barked.

"Fuck you," her mom said, turning on her heel and walking away.

Lily put a hand on Nico's arm. "It's okay," she told him. And then to her mom she called, "How much do you need?"

Taylor stopped and turned. "Three thousand. I'm behind on rent."

Lily nodded and pulled fifteen hundred in cash she still had left from her gambling winnings out of her purse and handed it over. "I'll transfer the rest to your account."

Taylor smiled, a feral smile. "Thanks, Lily, I could always count on you. I'll be in touch when the money clears." She walked off into the night on tottering heels.

Nico pulled her in for a hug. "Are you okay?"

She looked up at him. "I'm great. I just got a sister."

"You shouldn't have to bribe your own mother—"

She kissed him because she needed him just then. The solid strength of his body, the warmth of his touch. He slid his hand into her hair and kissed her in a tender way that somehow conveyed love.

She pulled back, choked up. "Let's have some fun, okay? I need some good memories of Vegas."

He slung an arm over her shoulders, and they headed back to the Strip. "Your wish is my command."

~ ~ ~

Nico woke on the floor of a huge hotel suite with a naked Lily wearing a small wedding veil sprawled on top of him. His head was pounding. This wasn't the room they'd checked into earlier. Bits and pieces of the night came back to him. Drinking, blackjack, Lily running and dancing by the fountain in front of the Bellagio until the security guard pulled her away, giggling like crazy. He did *not* get married. He'd never do that. He stared at the small white veil on her head and could think of no reasonable explanation.

"Lil." He shook her shoulders a little. "Wake up."

She tried to roll to her side and slipped right off him onto the floor. She landed on her back and let out a small snore. He stared at a butterfly tattoo under her belly button that hadn't been there before. Fuck. What had they done? He looked down at himself and found a matching imprint on his stomach, but faded. He scrubbed at it. Oh, thank God, it was one of those temporary tattoos. He was still wearing a condom. And the scary thing was he didn't even remember doing it. He got rid of that and returned to where Lily was sleeping on the floor.

"Lil." He gave her a nudge. "Wake up." She smiled in her sleep. He pulled her up to a sitting position, and she wrapped her arms around him and fell asleep on his chest. The woman slept like the dead. He gave up. He scooped her up and put her in the king-size canopied bed that seemed to be missing the blankets. He found them on the floor on the other side along with their clothes and a strip of condoms. He tucked the sheet and blanket over her and set the condoms on the nightstand.

Okay, okay. They probably just had a little fun last night. He pulled on his briefs and shorts and headed to the bathroom. Quickie weddings in Vegas could be undone quickly. They probably had quickie divorces too. Still, he felt jittery and sick. He peed like a racehorse, washed his hands, and then scrubbed at the butterfly on his stomach, managing to get it off. After he brushed his teeth with the complimentary toothbrush and toothpaste conveniently left in a basket on the counter, he called room service and ordered coffee and toast for both of them.

And then he waited, staring at his bride sleeping the morning away, her red hair bunched up in a tangle topped by the veil. Her lush mouth open slightly. Her shoulder was exposed, the skin perfect and smooth. The reason for her upset last night came back to him then clearly. Her mercenary mom only looking for money. She'd probably dropped the hint about a sister just to get more money out of Lily. Who knew if such a person even existed? And Lily, just accepting that was all she could expect from the woman. It physically hurt him to know that. Lily was such a good person inside and out with an exuberant, unsullied enjoyment of life. How could she have come from that woman? Or even her dad, who he knew to be a hard-ass. Maybe her dad was different in private with his daughter. He hoped so.

Room service arrived a short while later, and Lily jolted awake at the sharp knock on the door. "Who is it?" she asked, jackknifing up in bed. The sheet and blanket fell off her, and he rushed to cover her before the room-service guy could get an eyeful of beautiful breasts.

"Hey," he said gently, pushing her back down and covering her with the sheet and blanket. "It's room service. Keep covered for a minute."

She moaned. "I don't feel good."

He left her side to let room service in when Lily

leaped out of bed and raced to the bathroom, giving the room-service guy a nice streaking show.

Nico shrugged and gave him a tip. "Thanks. Sorry about that."

"Just a typical morning in Vegas for me," the guy said and then left.

The water was running in the bathroom, but he could still hear Lily retching. Better to get it out, he figured.

He sipped coffee and hoped like hell Lily had Advil or something like it in her suitcase. He looked around. It wasn't here. Their stuff must be in the first hotel room they'd checked into. Were they even in the same hotel? He heard her brushing her teeth. And then she stumbled from the bathroom and stood there naked in her veil, blue eyes wide.

"Did I get a tattoo?" she asked. "Twice?"

She turned and there on the dip in her lower back just above her curvy ass in big block letters was one word—Nico.

He leaped up and rubbed at his name. Oh, thank God. Another fake tattoo. If that had been real, every man she ever got naked with would see his name and—

"I'm afraid you did," he said. "It looks good, though."

"It says Nico!" she hollered, then winced. Her

hangover headache was probably much worse than his.

"Cool."

"Where's yours?"

He shrugged and turned his back to show her. She burst out laughing. "Yours says Lily."

"What?" He craned his neck to see over his shoulder. He couldn't see it. He headed to the bathroom and there it was, matching tattoos. At least he knew his was fake. "Huh."

"That's it? Huh? You're not upset to have my name permanently etched on your skin?"

"They did a good job. You got any Advil?"

She flounced out of the bathroom, making her breasts bounce. Shockingly, he wanted her. Headache and all. She located her purse and shook some pills out for him then washed a couple down for herself.

"I can't believe you let me get two tattoos," she said.

He wrapped his arms around her. "I like it."

She pulled away. "Ugh. This is awful." She snagged a white robe from the closet, slipped it on and sat at the small table where the coffee and toast were.

"Are we really married?" he asked, closing his eyes as he braced for the answer.

"What's wrong?" she snapped. "A tattoo is okay telling everyone you're mine, but a piece of paper saying so isn't?"

He opened his eyes. "Please tell me we're not married."

She threw a piece of toast at him. He ducked. She looked at her left hand and held it up to him. "Gold band. Where's yours?"

He checked. "I don't have one."

She dropped her head in her hands and the veil fell forward. "This doesn't make sense."

He shoved his hands in his pockets and met hard metal. He produced a gold band from his pocket. "Uh, Lily."

She lifted her head and stared at his ring. "Why weren't you wearing it and I was?"

He tried it on and it didn't fit. "Mine's too small."

"Mine's too big," she said, sliding it off. She gestured for his, they traded, and they both fit perfectly. "I think we are married," she said quietly.

His jaw dropped. That sucked. He was really shackled. And his family had missed it. He started pacing back and forth. He had to undo this, but he didn't want to hurt her feelings. He tried to remember the wedding and couldn't. Maybe it didn't really happen. Maybe they just dressed the part. He clung to that desperate line of thinking.

"Do you remember the wedding?" he asked.

"No." She took off the veil and set it on the table.

"Okay, okay, we would've needed a witness, right?

Who was the witness?" His voice was rising, and he forced it to a level tone. "There would be a license. We need to check! There's no need to panic yet."

She eyed him. "I'm not panicking. You are."

"You seriously want to be married to me?" he hollered. She winced, and he lowered his voice. He had to make her understand why this was never going to work. "The guy who fixes your dad's cars? I have nothing to offer you, and I sure as hell don't want to be married."

She scowled and stared at the veil. "Why not?"

He did not want to get into the whole mess with his ex. "Lil, you and I are from two different worlds. We both went into this with our eyes wide open. You don't want my kind of life, and I don't kid myself that I'd ever belong with the country-club set you come from."

She was quiet.

"After we shower and get rid of these hangovers," he said, "we'll retrace our steps and undo whatever needs undoing."

She finally met his eyes. "My dad wanted me to marry Trevor."

"Who the hell is that?"

She rubbed her temples. "He's one of those pink-shirted country-club guys, Harvard alum, old money. Blah, blah, blah. We're practically brother and sister."

He leaned both hands on the table and said in a deceptively soft voice because he wanted to yell, "Are you engaged?"

"No."

He straightened, not wanting to think too hard on why he was so relieved when he personally didn't want to be married.

"We'll fix this," he said firmly and headed for the shower. Then he did a quick about-face, snagged the veil, and took it with him. It was freaking him out. He tossed it in the bathroom trash can and decided to deal with it all later once they'd both had a chance to get rid of their killer hangovers. When he got out a long while later, he'd calmed down.

He wrapped a towel around his waist and went back into the suite, where Lily was standing in that white robe, looking out the floor-to-ceiling windows at the skyline. They must be in the penthouse suite because the view was spectacular. He couldn't resist coming up behind her and sliding his arms around her. The tattoo with his name would wash off in the shower, and he wanted her to be only his for a little longer. "You know what's cool about your tattoo?" he asked in her ear before biting gently on her earlobe.

"What?" she asked softly just as he slipped the robe from her shoulders. "Nico!"

He wrapped one arm around her waist. "Exactly."

She squirmed, wiggling her ass against him. "We're in front of the window!"

He turned and pulled her with him to the bed. He laid her on her belly, and then pulled her up by the hips so he had easy access and a nice view of his name. He took off his towel, snagged a condom from the nightstand, and rolled it on.

"I want to see and hear my name," he said, his hand slipping around to stroke her. She moaned. He wouldn't let her wash this off. He loved his name there.

"I'm glad you have a Lily tattoo," she said in a breathy voice. "You're mine forever."

Sweat broke out on his forehead. He dropped his hand and leaned back, but then she spread her legs wider, and he felt himself grow even harder.

"Take me," she said.

He surged forward, taking what was his, with one swift, hard thrust. She cried out his name, which only made him want more, made him crazed to hear it.

"More," he growled as he gripped her hips and took her fierce and deep. She chanted his name, gasping it out as he took her like a damned animal, until they were both drenched in sweat. He reached around and stroked her quickly, and she screamed her release, which sent him right over as her body clenched around him. He collapsed finally at her side, one hand possessively across her lower back right on his name.

He closed his eyes as it hit him that he couldn't have it both ways. Couldn't make her be only his and hold himself back. He had to give. He just wasn't sure he could. Marriage was one line he couldn't cross.

CHAPTER FOURTEEN

Lily let the hot shower work its magic while she tried to sort through her tangled-up emotions. It really hurt the way Nico looked so horrified at the thought of being married to her. Like it was the world's worst thing that had ever happened to him. For her, it wasn't, though. She understood what he meant about them coming from two different worlds, but she'd never fit into the country-club mold either. She'd always felt on the outside. She could see herself with Nico, who was unlike anyone she'd ever known, but in a good way.

Her shoulders slumped as it hit her that she was in love with him. What had she gone and done? She couldn't be in love with Nico. He clearly didn't see marriage in his future, but she wanted that. Marriage and kids, the chance to make her own loving family. She'd never had that, and she wanted it very much. She washed herself briskly and glanced down at her stomach to see the butterfly tattoo was fading. She scrubbed a little harder, and it faded a little more. Nico lied! No wonder he'd been so weird about her taking a shower. He kept pulling her back to bed, distracting her with his hands and mouth. The man had made her come seven times. She'd finally made her escape when his cell rang. She scrubbed at her back, hoping the Nico tattoo was coming off too. It was tough to see back there. How dare he!

A flash of memory came to her. An Elvis impersonator. Maybe that was their witness. Maybe there was a fake tattoo store near the chapel. Why would Nico want his name on her back if he didn't want a future with her? She finished in the shower, wrapped a towel around her, and stepped into the room.

He turned. "I put your casino check in your purse. I can't believe it was still in my wallet after last night. Speaking of which—"

She held up a hand. "The tattoos washed off."

He looked sheepish. "Guess it had to happen."

She jammed her hands on her hips. "Why did you let me freak out that I was permanently inked?"

He shrugged. "I liked my name on you."

"Why?"

He didn't reply.

She crossed to him and met his dark brown eyes.

"Your name on my back says something permanent between us, yet you're panicking that we're married." Her throat got tight. "Is it really so bad being married to me?"

"Don't cry," he said.

Her lower lip wobbled. "I'm not crying."

He cupped her jaw with one large warm hand and met her eyes with a tender gaze. "Anyone would be lucky to be married to you."

She dashed away an errant tear. "Really?"

"Sure."

"Even you?"

He dropped his hand and didn't answer.

"Except you," she said.

"Not me," he said, "but that's nothing to do with you. I just…I'm never getting married again."

"You were married before?"

"Yes."

"What happened?"

His lips formed a grim line.

"What happened?" she pressed.

He blew out a breath. "I'm not good at it."

She recognized a lame excuse when she heard it. She reached for her tough, stoic side. The stiff upper lip her dad had drilled into her. "Don't be such a weak female," her dad would say when faced with her tears. And when she couldn't stop crying, he'd say with disgust, "Spencers don't cry," before leaving the room. She pulled off her wedding band and stashed it in her purse. Nico wasn't wearing his anyway. They'd undo this, as he said.

"There was an Elvis impersonator," she said, turning back to him. "Maybe he was the witness."

"I found the marriage license in your purse," he said.

Her eyes widened. "You did?"

He smiled. "Yeah. I called the Marriage License Bureau. Nothing was filed for our marriage record. So maybe it's just the license. Not an actual marriage."

"Or maybe the chapel just hasn't filed it yet. Maybe what's in my purse is just a copy."

He stopped smiling, and her heart sank.

She held up a hand. "You know what? Just pretend it never happened." She quickly got dressed in her clothes from the day before, feeling Nico's eyes on her.

Her cell rang. She took a deep breath and went to answer it, pulling it from her purse. "It's my dad," she whispered.

He kept quiet.

"Hello?" she said in a low voice.

Her dad immediately started reaming her out. She pulled the phone away from her ear. "He's mad," she whispered.

Nico raised his brows in a gesture of no kidding.

She put the phone back to her ear. "Dad, please stop yelling. It's very hard to understand you when you yell." She listened with a sinking feeling and finally said the only thing she could say in the face of the mess she'd made. "I'll take care of everything." He harassed her some more about the bar exam and when she was going to get her ass home. "I'll be home next weekend." He hung up.

"What'd he say?"

She tossed her cell in her purse and met his eyes, suddenly exhausted. "Apparently I was very busy making phone calls last night after I got married."

"Does he know it's me?"

She gave him a look. "He says I told him to call me Mrs. Nico Marino from now on. This was a shock to hear at three a.m. because he thought I was in Boston with a friend taking a bar exam review course, and he'd already picked out the man I'm supposed to marry, who is not his mechanic."

"Call him back and tell him we're not married."

"I don't know if we're married!" She took a deep breath. "Not only that, I left a message on our lawyer's voicemail asking for one hundred thousand dollars to be sent to my new husband's business and to work up the paperwork to make him full owner."

"Lily! Why would you do that?"

"Because, according to my dad, I said being a full

owner was what you wanted most in the world and it was my job as your wife to make your dreams come true. So I solved all your problems and now you just have to help me solve mine."

"What's your problem? Other than being married to me."

She huffed. "I need to find my sister."

Nico rubbed the back of his neck. "I should've stuck to beer last night. I can't believe you paid off my debt. I was supposed to earn that myself."

She went on. "No prenup, of course, since it was so fast. Dad was especially thrilled about that part."

He jabbed a finger at her. "I'm paying you back, Lil. Come on. We're retracing our steps and we're fixing this."

She followed him out the door, dragging her feet. It didn't matter anyway. If they were married, they'd get it undone. If they weren't married, it was the same result—Nico wouldn't be part of her future. All of her stupid loving feelings wouldn't be returned. When had they ever? She'd never felt loved and accepted by anyone. Her dad never said he loved her, his disappointment in her was always crystal clear, her stepmom barely tolerated her, her mom only wanted money from her. That was why she'd wanted to meet her sister so much. A sibling who'd also been given up would understand like no one else in the world could.

Nico grabbed her hand and pulled her along. He couldn't wait to get to the bottom of this mystery and make sure he wasn't shackled to her. He punched the button for the elevator. "We just need to find the chapel with the Elvis impersonator."

"I'm sure there's more than one."

He narrowed his eyes. "Then we'll check all of them."

"I thought you were in a hurry to get home," she said.

"Now I'm in a hurry to fix my life."

She clamped her mouth shut and stared straight ahead. He left her alone. Her cell rang as they crossed the hotel lobby. She held up a finger to Nico and moved to a quiet corner. It was her mom.

"Hi, Taylor."

Her mom confirmed the money had arrived and was now prattling on happily about how she wanted to decorate her kitchen with new curtains.

"I need the name and phone number of my sister."

"I don't think it's a good idea," her mom said. "She's very angry."

"At you! We had a deal. What's her name?"

At her rising voice, Nico moved to stand near her.

"Calm down." Taylor let out a huge sigh. "They called her Missy."

"Short for what? Melissa?"

"Yes."

"Okay, last name." She tried to control her temper. It was always like this trying to get anything from her mom. She was so withholding with information, affection, everything. She'd never given Lily anything without her working for it and paying dearly.

"Last I heard she'd married a man named Braxton. But I think they divorced."

"I need a phone number. An address. Something."

"I could use a new car," Taylor said.

Anger and a crushing disappointment washed through her. "After you tell me everything you know about Missy."

"There's this cute convertible. A real bargain at twenty-five thousand."

"Done. But first I need the information."

Her mom let out another huge sigh like Lily was just an inconvenient bump on the path to more money. "I don't know much. She used to live in L.A. When she was married. She could be anywhere."

"Where did you last hear from her?"

"Seattle."

"When?"

"A few months ago. She called and told me to stop sending her birthday cards."

Lily felt a pang of envy. Taylor had never sent her

anything. But maybe that was part of the deal with her dad. No contact.

"And you don't know her last name?" Lily asked.

"Her adoptive family was Higgins."

Finally. Some real information she could use. "How old is she?"

"I had her when I was sixteen. You do the math."

Her sister was two years older than her. "Anything else you can tell me?"

"That's all I know. She's bitter and angry. You won't like her—"

"Thank you. I'll wire you the money." She punched the button to end the call.

Nico looked at her, his deep brown eyes full of pity. "You're not sending her more money, are you? She's just using you."

She lifted her chin. "What would you do, huh? Just never meet your own sister?"

"Don't send her any more money," he said.

"I keep my promises," she said.

He shook his head, and they headed outside. "Let's try the most famous wedding chapel first. Most likely two drunk idiots like us just went to the obvious choice."

She couldn't even protest the label. She was an idiot. For loving him. For screwing up her life and his. Augh.

They walked for a bit and stopped at a chapel that wasn't the most famous, but she thought she recognized the life-size cutout of Elvis in the front window. The clerk had no record of them. Next they went to the most famous chapel, A Little White Chapel, with a big sign boasting that Joan Collins and Michael Jordan had married there (though not to each other).

Nico went stock-still. "I remember this sign with the twenty-four-hour drive-through wedding." He blew out a breath. "Here goes."

He led the way, stopping in front of the clerk, a white-haired woman with her hair teased into a bouffant. Her name tag read Shirley.

"Hi, Shirley," Nico said. "Do you have any record of Nico Marino and Lily Spencer here last night?"

Shirley clapped her hands, looking delighted to see them. "You're back! Wonderful! Now, Elvis is off duty—" she lowered her voice "—he had a root canal." She beamed. "But we still have a number of lovely packages you might like. How about a Hawaiian theme?" She looked from Lily to Nico eagerly.

"So we didn't go through with it?" Lily asked.

Shirley shook her head. "You were a little worse for the wear, but I could just see the love shining in your eyes. I knew you'd be back!"

Nico met Lily's eyes, looking serious. Their gazes

locked and all Lily could think was that maybe their drunken selves knew more about what they really felt for one another than their sober selves could admit. Maybe their drunken selves didn't care where they came from or how different they were. Maybe their drunken, idiotic selves knew what they were doing to bring them here. And just maybe Nico didn't hate the idea of marriage as much as he said.

Nico swallowed visibly and turned to Shirley. "Exactly what happened?"

Shirley tsked. "You don't remember? You came in here all ready to go. Well, *she* was. She had the veil and ring on already, and she was waving the license around, singing she was 'Mrs. Nicky Malino.'"

"Nico Marino," Lily said softly.

"Yes!" Shirley exclaimed. "And Nico kept saying that you needed the cookies. But I'm sure he meant cake. Anyway, you ordered the Elvis special and just when it was time to say the vows, you—" she pointed at Nico "—grabbed your fiancée, threw her over your shoulder, and took off."

Lily studied Nico. She'd thought he'd laugh or look relieved, but instead he was serious, his dark brown eyes searching hers.

Shirley went on. "I kept calling after you, telling you it wasn't official until we had the ceremony, and I needed the license to file after the ceremony, but you'd moved on." She smiled at both of them. "So, what should we go with today?"

"We won't be needing your services," Nico said, "but thank you."

They stepped back outside. Lily put on her dark shades, glad for the cover from the tears she felt threatening.

"I guess it's for the better," she said.

Nico turned to her. "It is for the better." He jabbed a finger back at the chapel. "That would've been a huge mistake."

She swallowed. "Yup."

"Be honest," he snapped. "Did you ever see yourself marrying a guy like me?"

"I never met a guy like you," she replied honestly.

His jaw clenched. "Everything worked out as it should. C'mon, let's go find our luggage and get out of this hellhole."

~ ~ ~

Nico didn't know what to make of this eerily quiet Lily. They were on the road to L.A., and she'd been blankly staring out the window for more than an hour. She wasn't listening to her audio lectures either. They'd agreed it was a good thing they weren't married for real, so everything should've gone back to normal. But somehow it hadn't. He'd thought he'd feel nothing but relief, but instead he just felt pissed off. Which was just stupid. This was never supposed to be more than a two-week fling. He had nothing to offer someone like Lily. Of course she'd never met a guy like him in her fancy private schools or country-club parties. What did he care if he wasn't some rich, pink-shirted golf junkie. He didn't even want to be married!

In any case, he knew their fuckup wasn't what was upsetting her. It was the whole deal with her sister. She'd poked around on the Internet and made some calls earlier only to discover that her sister's adoptive parents had died in a car accident. She'd left messages on three Melissa Higginses' voicemails in Seattle and had heard nothing back. She hadn't found a Melissa or Missy Braxton anywhere.

He finally broke the silence, his concern for her overriding his bad mood. "Hey, I'm sure you'll find your sister. Maybe you can hire a private investigator. They're good at tracking people down."

"Maybe," she said in a subdued voice.

He couldn't stand to have her so miserable. "Is there anything I can do to cheer you up?"

"You could get me a new family. Mine sucks."

"Maybe you'd like mine. Bunch of brothers, a dad, a great stepmom."

"What about your mom?"

He blew out a breath. "She died when I was seven."

"Oh, I'm sorry."

"It's all right. She was great from what I remember. So's my stepmom. You should meet her." He glanced over to find her frowning.

"You mean when we get back to Connecticut?" she asked.

"Yeah."

"We're not married, so you're off the hook. No strings, remember?"

"It doesn't have to be that way." He could hardly believe he'd said that, but once the words were out, he really meant it. He didn't want to say goodbye. He wasn't ready. Not yet.

She looked at him, but he couldn't read her expression with the shades covering her eyes. "You said you're never getting married again, but I want that. Marriage and kids are important to me. I want a chance to make a loving family of my own." Her voice got choked up, and he tensed, worried she was going to bawl in his truck. It pained him to see her cry. She blew out a breath. "I never had that, as you've seen, and I want it. There's no point in us continuing. We want different things."

She was right. They wanted different things. She deserved to have everything she wanted.

"You going to marry some country-club guy?" he asked.

She laughed mirthlessly. Kinda sad, even, for a laugh. "I'll probably marry someone I meet in the city. Lots of single twenty-somethings there."

He was in his thirties. She should be with someone her age. "How many kids you planning on?"

"I was an only child, well, I was raised as one. I don't know, three. Maybe four."

"You'd better get started, then. You're already twenty-five."

She huffed. "Thank you for reminding me of my old age."

"You're not old. I'm just saying it takes time to have four kids."

She was quiet.

"I wish you luck," he said. "I'm sure you'll be a great mom."

"It would help if I had an example of a great mom," she muttered.

"You should meet my stepmom."

"I'm not meeting your family! Remember? You don't want to be tied down. This is a two-week thing."

"We still have one more week," he pointed out.

"Oh, goody."

"What's that supposed to mean?"

She crossed her arms. "I think one week is plenty."

"What are you pissed at me for?"

"I'm sorry. I'm just upset. We'll screw as much as you want."

"Don't be like that." He glanced over to find her lower lip trembling. He took her hand and held it, offering the only comfort he could. She was quiet the rest of the drive.

He just wished there was something he could do.

~ ~ ~

Nico followed Lily into her grandfather's house in L.A. She already had the key. The small ranch home was hot and smelled old and musty. He helped her open all the windows to air the place out, and they cranked the air-conditioning.

Lily opened the door near the kitchen that led to the garage. "There it is," she said in a flat tone, "all yours."

He stepped inside the garage, and she left. He circled the car, a black 1969 Mustang Boss 429e. Pure euphoria shot through him. It was the ultimate barn find. He could restore this car to its former glory and some collector would snap it up. A layer of dust coated the car. Untouched. He sucked in a breath. The odometer had five hundred miles on it. He could sell it for six hundred thousand easy. Maybe more. He peered in the backseat. There was still plastic on the seatbelts. He could buy out Kevin and have enough left over for a house.

It was the find of a lifetime.

Only his euphoria was short-lived, replaced by an overwhelming sense of loss. This was why they'd made the trip. He'd gotten what he'd wanted and now there was nothing to do but the long drive home. Every day bringing them closer to goodbye, every night bittersweet as the end drew near. Dammit. How could he have everything he'd ever wanted and still not feel satisfied?

Because all he could think about was Lily sitting in the house, miserable, and going through her grandfather's things. He wanted to take away her pain, make all her dreams come true, but he couldn't.

He raised the garage door and stepped out into the sunshine, pacing a bit on the front sidewalk. It had to be the road trip that made him feel this strong connection to her. He'd just met her two weeks ago. One week on the road together had been intense, but soon they'd go back to their real lives, go their separate ways, and they'd both be better off for it.

He imagined that future. He'd pay her for the Mustang, restore and sell it, and finally be full owner in his shop. He'd become a true success from his own hard work. Lily would become a lawyer in the city and meet some twenty-something professional guy who didn't have to get his hands dirty for a living. She'd have kids and make the loving family she'd always wanted. That was as it should be. Lily and some guy that was perfect husband material.

Nico wasn't that guy.

~ ~ ~

Lily went through her grandfather's things, though there wasn't much. The house was neat with very little clutter. Her grandfather either lived frugally, or he threw away a lot of stuff. The kitchen and living room had nothing personal in them, so she headed for the bedroom. She found some pictures in a nightstand drawer of a German shepherd that he clearly missed. She moved to the closet and found a large shoe box on a shelf. She snagged the box that still had the label for the hiking boots that had been inside. She settled cross-legged on the floor and carefully sifted through it.

There were medals from when her grandfather was in the marines. He'd been Special Forces, and she suspected he suffered from PTSD. Her mom had said only that he was horrible and drunk most of the time. There was a collection of birthday cards from her grandmother, who died when her mom was twelve.

She found a picture of her grandfather as a child with what appeared to be his brother. Another family member Lily had never met. She kept going and found a stack of honor roll certificates with her mom's name on them. She hadn't known Taylor was good at school. What happened? Why had she gone straight to Vegas to be a showgirl?

She thought more about her mom's life. Taylor had no mom to get her through her teen years. She had a harsh father that she couldn't depend on. And no siblings to lean on. She supposed Taylor could've ended up worse than she had.

She found some more pictures at the bottom of the box. Her mom as a baby. Her mom at about seven scowling at the camera, another closer to ten looking off in the distance, another as a teen staring right at the camera with a defiant look on her face. She'd grown tough over the years. And looked miserable. She put everything back in the box. Her work was done here. She got what little she could. Nico got his car. There was nothing to do but leave.

A pang of longing went through her. How much better would it have been if she'd found her sister? If they'd had a reunion. She decided to fly to Seattle. She'd investigate in person if there was a Melissa Higgins living there. She didn't want to go home with nothing but a shoe box.

Nico appeared in the doorway. "Hey. How's it going?"

"Not much here," she said. "I'm just going to take this box and put the house up for sale. How was the car?"

He grinned. "Great! She's worth a fortune."

He looked so happy. Well, he got what he wanted. At least one of them had.

"I figure I can get six hundred grand easy," Nico went on. "Name your price."

She waved that away. "It's yours." She stood. "As thanks for the company. I'm going to Seattle after this and then I'll fly home."

His brows drew together. "That's it? Thanks for the company? You said we'd have two weeks together. I only got one week."

"Things changed. Besides, we both knew this wasn't for the long haul. Now you have the car. I'm going to find my sister."

He crossed to her, set the box she was holding on the floor, and wrapped his arms around her. His voice dropped a register, low and coaxing. "I'll drive with you to Seattle."

She shook her head. "Let's not make this any more difficult than it has to be. Okay?"

He dropped his arms and stepped back. "Just because I don't want to marry you doesn't mean…"

Her throat tightened. "What?"

"It doesn't mean I don't care about you."

"I'll always remember our time together fondly," she said softly.

He scowled. "Dammit, Lil!"

She startled at the unexpected harshness in his tone.

He jabbed a hand in the air. "It was a helluva lot more than fond!"

"We both knew it would come to this," she said quietly.

He glared for a moment and then started talking in a calm, steady voice. "We talked *a lot*. We ate three meals a day together. We looked at weird-ass things in weird-ass places. We faced your fears together. We almost died leaping from a plane—"

"We didn't—"

"Don't interrupt me! We shared three feet of cab space all day every day! We shared a hotel room every night, whether or not we were naked. I was your second, and I wish I'd been your first so you never would've had a moment's doubt about how damn sexy you are." He crossed his arms and finished with the most embarrassing thing of all. "And I kissed your pooch."

She sucked in a breath. "Don't talk about my pooch." She'd go on a diet immediately.

"I love your pooch."

Her eyes watered. Why was he making this so

hard? "You do not."

"I do!"

"You do not!"

"I do too!"

"That's crazy!" She looked away. "You're crazy."

And then he pulled her into his arms. He kissed her soft and tender, and she clung to him as her mind went blank and there was nothing but his strong arms holding her, pressing her close as his mouth claimed hers. Her body responded immediately, heating against him. He lowered her to the bed, already pulling up her shirt, and she suddenly remembered where they were.

"Nico, we can't do this here."

He undid the front clasp of her bra and nuzzled into her cleavage.

"Please," she said. And then he was suckling her breast and a familiar tug of desire arced through her. Heat pooled between her legs. "Not here," she said weakly.

He groaned and put her bra back together. Then he pulled her up off the bed. "C'mon. Let's go check in at the hotel."

He tugged her toward the door.

"Wait, I need the box."

He scooped it up, and she followed him outside, where he set the box in the back of the Mustang and then set everything up to tow the car. It took a while and the more time that passed, the more doubts began to settle in. What was she doing prolonging things between them?

She watched him putting the flatbed truck into position, lowering the back, making a ramp for the car. Then he undid a long cable from the back of the truck. By the time he'd gotten the car in place, she was resolved to end things before they both got hurt.

CHAPTER FIFTEEN

"Get in," Nico said in a harsh voice because Lily was just standing there in the driveway, blinking rapidly like she wanted to cry, which made him tense and angry because he felt like howling. The writing was on the wall. It was almost time for goodbye. But he didn't want to say goodbye. He wanted more time. Not forever. Just another few weeks. Maybe just until she moved to the city to start her new job.

She got in, put on her seatbelt, and slid on her shades. "Well, you got your car."

"Yup."

"So…I, um, I think it might be easier—"

"You owe me." She was not dumping him when they both knew they weren't done.

Her jaw dropped. "How do I owe you? I gave you the car—"

"I thought you were smart."

"I am smart," she snapped. Good, she was getting

mad too. Now they could have a good fight about it and make up in bed.

"Then stop acting like you don't know what I mean. I get six more days. Then I have to go to my brother's bachelor party."

"But I'm not driving back home. I'm going to—"

"Six days! Six nights! That was the fucking deal."

"Nico," she said gently, which made him feel kind of desperate. He was losing her and there wasn't a damn thing he could do about it.

"We'll talk at the hotel," he said because at least there he could remind her why they deserved to have six more nights together. If that was all he could get, he'd take it.

Her cell rang in her purse. "It's my dad," she muttered.

He grunted.

Lily listened for a long while before exclaiming, "No! That's not what really hap—" She got quiet. "He hung up."

He glanced over to find her pale. "What? What happened?"

"He…oh, God, Nico. I'm so sorry. I'll try to fix it."

A sick feeling washed over him, and he pulled to the side of the road. Luckily, they hadn't gotten on the freeway yet. "What happened?"

"He was furious about the marriage without a prenup. He thinks you corrupted me, seducing me into shirking my responsibilities and screwing your way into the family money. God, I should've called him back yesterday and told him we weren't really married, but I was upset, and now I ruined everything!"

"What? What did you ruin?"

"He blacklisted your shop. Told everyone he knows that you aren't to be trusted."

"Okay, wait. So…I lost him as a client, and you're telling me…" He couldn't even say the words, but he knew. George Spencer was a powerful man with a wide sphere of influence.

"He's turned the wealthy families in our area against you. No one will cross him."

"Great," he muttered. "What am I supposed to do, start over in California? Call him back right now and explain it. Tell him we're not married and it was all a misunderstanding. And you'd better tell him to straighten out that lie about me too. I'm not leaving my home because some uppity prick thinks money gives him the right to ruin someone just because they fucked their daughter."

"Is that what this was? Fucking the client's daughter?"

He was too furious to answer.

Her lips formed a flat line. "You know what? Forget it. You said it perfectly. I'll try again after we get to the hotel, though God knows if he'll listen to me. I might've forgot to mention I'm the black sheep of the family. I've disappointed him from the moment I was born."

He pulled back on the road, puzzling over that last bit. How could she have disappointed when she was just a baby? Her family was seriously screwed up, and he had a whole new appreciation for his. He should've known better than to get involved with George Spencer's daughter. Now instead of earning full ownership in his shop, he was facing shutting it down. This whole thing had been a mistake from the very beginning.

~ ~ ~

They drove to the hotel in silence. Lily checked them into the Beverly Hills Wilshire, her favorite hotel because they'd filmed *Pretty Woman* there. She loved the fairy-tale movie where both the hero and heroine rescued each other. She sighed. Staying here was as close as she'd get to a fairy tale in her life. Nico was tense, his jaw clenched as they rode the elevator to their room.

After their luggage was brought up, Lily sat at the large mahogany desk and called her dad again while

Nico paced the room like a caged panther. Her dad was being completely unreasonable. He was trying to punish her by punishing Nico. She explained that they weren't really married, and he believed her, but he also believed that Nico had put her future in jeopardy by taking her halfway across the country when she should've been studying for the bar. Not only that, he believed Nico sweet-talked her into paying off his debt. And that she was in danger of giving him a blank check.

No amount of explaining on her part made a dent in her dad's outrage and lack of faith in her. And then he hung up on her. Again.

"That went well," she told Nico.

He let out something alarmingly close to a growl.

"He, uh, he's just mad. He'll cool off, and I'll try again tomorrow."

"Great," Nico bit out. "I have to call the shop."

He called the guy he'd left in charge of the shop to warn him, and told him to keep him updated. Lily looked up flights to Seattle on her cell. She found a flight for the next morning. After he hung up, she turned to him.

"I can catch a nine a.m. flight to Seattle tomorrow morning," she said.

He stalked toward her. "You're not flying to Seattle tomorrow."

She stood so he wouldn't be towering over her. "You don't have to drive me. I'll take a cab to the airport."

He stopped in front of her. "I can't believe this. You ruined me! And then you just take off?"

That stung because, even though she hadn't meant to ruin him, somehow the whole thing had snowballed into a huge disastrous mess.

"I'll bet you wish you never met me," she said in a strained voice. She cleared her throat, stronger now, and threw her hair over her shoulder. "But I'm glad I met you. You showed me what a fling is like, and you know what? It sucks!" Her voice rose in volume at her aggravation over feeling so much for a man who would never love her back.

"This whole thing was a mistake right from the beginning!" he roared. "I got the wrong redhead!"

"I'm never having a fling again! The next time—"

She was cut off by a hard kiss. His hand gripped her hair; the other hand cupped her firmly between the legs, making her gasp. Suddenly they were frantically pulling at each other's clothes and kissing like their next breath depended on it. Her shirt flew off as she struggled with his. He yanked off his T-shirt and flung open her bra, his mouth slamming into hers again. The button flew off her shorts as he yanked them off, and then he ripped her panties. She stood there naked and shocked. He was breathing hard, his gaze hungry as he slid off his briefs. She took in his massive erection, and they slammed together again, tongues sparring, their bodies straining to get closer. His teeth sank into her lower lip, making her whimper. He released her lip only long enough to maneuver her toward the bed, then their mouths fused together as he backed her up until her legs hit the side of the bed, and he landed on top of her. They rolled crazily, kissing and touching everywhere at once, and then he pinned her beneath him, his mouth moving to her neck as his hand slid lower, his fingers thrusting inside, making her dizzy with want.

He claimed her mouth again, rough and urgent. And she kissed him back, feeling desperate, knowing this was their last time together. Her body craved the closeness she couldn't get with his heart. And then he thrust inside, the heat and thickness of him filling her, stretching her. She moaned at the incredible feeling. Then she realized why it felt different.

She tore her mouth from his. "Condom," she gasped out.

"Oh, fuck," he muttered. He left to get one, and she sat up, pulling the sheet up to her neck, cooling off from the craziness. What was she doing hopping into bed with him? This was only going to make things worse.

He rolled it on and strode toward her, apparently not liking what he saw. He ripped the sheet off her and pulled her right out of bed.

"This is what a fling feels like," he told her just before his mouth slammed over hers. He hauled her to the wall, one arm banded around her waist, and pressed his hard body against hers. When he finally let her up for air, she couldn't speak because he overwhelmed her, nipping and kissing her neck, his stubble scraping against the delicate skin. He moved up to her ear, licking the delicate shell before biting down on her earlobe. "It's rough and raw," he growled just as he lifted her and thrust inside.

She sucked in a breath at the sudden invasion and wrapped her legs around him. He pounded into her, the wall cool and hard at her back, and she just let go, exhilarated by what she'd brought out in him even as she was dimly aware that he'd shown her only tenderness before. He kept going and the pressure escalated, her insides tightening, making her tremble on the edge of release.

He gripped her hair suddenly and pulled back enough to look in her eyes, his expression fierce. "You fucking *ruined* me," he said in a rough voice that shook her to her core because his eyes said love.

"You ruined me too!" she cried, meaning love with all her heart.

And then he pushed her over the edge, slamming into her again with a hard thrust, his mouth swallowing her scream, utterly destroying her. She'd gained and lost everything all at the same time.

CHAPTER SIXTEEN

Nico was having the most delicious dream. His cock deep in Lily's mouth, those plump pink lips surrounding him, sucking him dry. He woke with a start as soft hair teased across his stomach. He opened his eyes to find that fantasy was real, that mouth that he'd dreamed about for so long on him, and she was so-o-oo good at it. He jerked and tried to hold back, but it was no good, he exploded with shocking intensity. Aftershocks pulsed through him as she took him until he had nothing left, swallowing down every last drop and licking him clean.

He jerked as her pink tongue rasped over him. "Lily," he groaned.

She looked up at him with those electric blue eyes. "I'll never forget you, Nico," she said, rolling away from him. He grabbed her and hauled her on top of him, wishing things were different.

He pushed her soft red hair back from her face and

cradled her cheek with one hand. "Just a little longer."

She buried her face in his neck and hugged him. He heard a sniffle and blinked back the annoying wetness in his own eyes.

"I'll drive you to the airport," he said gruffly. "Don't take a cab."

"Okay," she mumbled against his neck. He held her for a long time, not ready to say goodbye. But finally they had to go. She squeezed him one last time; then she went to get ready.

By the time they were both ready, Nico was on edge. This didn't feel right. He should go with her to Seattle. What was she going to do, wander around the city by herself knocking on doors? Either way, fly or drive to Seattle, he'd have to leave the Mustang behind and pay one of his guys to fly out and drive it back. He didn't have enough time to make the side trip and get home in time for Vince's wedding.

She pulled her cell out and checked it. "Oh! There's a message from someone in Seattle." A wide smile broke out on her face as she listened to the message, and she quickly dialed.

"Hi, it's Lily." A pause. "I'm the other daughter she gave up."

Lily listened for a moment. "I'm flying to Seattle to see you. Is that okay?" There was a pause. "I have a box of our grandfather's things, including pictures of

Taylor growing up. I'll show you." She laughed. "I don't like her much either." She bounced a little in place. "Okay, I'll see you soon."

She hung up. "I have a sister. A big sister!"

"That's great," he said, really meaning it.

"She's going to pick me up at the airport. She hates Taylor too."

"Then it's unanimous."

"Ah!" she shrieked. "I can't believe I found her."

He tried to match her enthusiasm even as he realized she didn't need him. She'd found her sister. That was the important thing. He hugged her and kissed her hair. "I'm happy for you. We'd better get going."

She nodded happily and grabbed her suitcase.

Nico drove her to the airport, listening to her babble on about what she imagined her sister would be like, wondering if she had the red hair too, and what they'd do together in Seattle. He loved seeing her so happy, even if he felt like crap. Because they both knew this was goodbye, but only he was the one dreading it.

They were nearly at the airport when her cell rang. "Hello!" she answered cheerfully. She immediately got serious. "What? What do you mean?" A long silence. "Okay, then. Bye."

She hung up and got quiet. He glanced over to

find her glassy-eyed and pale.

"What happened? Who was that?" he asked.

"That was my father's lawyer. He…"

"What?" he barked. "What did he do now?"

Her voice came out small. "He disowned me."

"He can't do that!"

Her voice came out in a harsh whisper. "He said my trust fund was the last penny I'd ever get. He doesn't trust me with the Spencer legacy because of my recent activities."

Her father meant him. Dammit. She wasn't going to lose everything because of him.

She turned to him, her eyes shiny with unshed tears, which made his chest ache something fierce. "He never loved me."

"He's your dad. He has to love you."

"No one ever has," she said before she quietly broke down in tears.

He wanted to say he loved her, but the words stuck in his throat. Because it wasn't fair to her. He couldn't back it up with the kind of forever commitment she craved. That she deserved.

They drove the rest of the way to the airport in awkward silence. Tears silently streamed down Lily's face, and he felt so helpless, all he could do was hold her hand. He was going to kill her father for putting her through this. Especially when she'd been so happy to find her sister. Disowning his only daughter! What an asshole. He would fix this as soon as he got back home face to face.

He pulled up to departures, stopped at the curb, and fetched her luggage from the back of the truck for her. She met him at the curb.

"You still want to go?" he asked.

She wiped her tears away and took a deep breath. "Of course. She's all I got left."

"Text me when you get there, okay?"

She nodded once and kissed his cheek. "Bye, Nico."

"Your dad will come around. I'm sure of it."

"Say goodbye," she said.

"I don't want to say goodbye. I hate goodbyes."

She looked up at him, her electric blue eyes still shiny with tears. "I need you to. Please."

He grabbed her and kissed her one last time, a quick, hard goodbye. Then he turned and got in the truck without a backward glance.

And that was the end of the most heart-wrenching, fucked-up week of his entire life. His throat felt tight, his chest ached, everything about this felt wrong. This was exactly what he'd been trying to avoid. It was his own damn fault. He'd been stupid enough to let her in close.

As he headed back home, he channeled all of his

aggravation and hurt into payback to her father. He got in touch with Luke and told him to pass along the message that he'd be home for Vince's bachelor party and to get Gabe ready to lawyer up against the bastard George Spencer. He'd be damned if Lily was going to lose everything because of him. And no way in hell was he going to be blacklisted into bankruptcy.

~ ~ ~

Lily had never cried so much in her life. Losing Nico, having her father disown her, it was all too much. This had been both the best and worst week of her life.

By the time the announcement came over the plane's speakers that they'd be landing shortly, she forced herself to pull it together. She was about to meet her sister for the first time, and she didn't want to look like a red-eyed red-haired lunatic. She touched up her makeup and prayed that this went well. She couldn't handle even one more upset at this point. She'd have a complete breakdown.

Finally, they landed and she followed the long line of passengers to baggage claim, where Missy had said to meet her. She searched the faces of every woman she passed, wondering how she'd know. Maybe Missy would know to look for red hair. She should've sent her a picture. Her breath caught, and she stopped short.

Her sister was holding up a sign that read Lily, long-lost sister.

"That's me!" she cried. "It's me, Missy!"

She raced into Missy's open arms. They started hugging and crying at the same time.

"I've always wanted a sister," Lily choked out.

"Me too," her sister said. They laughed and cried some more and then stared at each other in wonder. They didn't look much alike. Her sister had brown hair and brown eyes, and she was shorter and not busting with curves like Lily. But they had the same big lips with the little dip at the top. Taylor's lips.

Missy shook her head. "Come on, we're making a scene."

They wiped their eyes and went to get Lily's luggage from the baggage carousel.

"I knew you had to be the real deal as soon as I saw that hair," Missy said. "I dye mine brown. It's red too."

"Really?"

"Yeah. But I didn't want to look like *her,* so I got rid of it."

"I only just found out about you, or I would've been in touch sooner."

Her sister gave her a small smile. "I only just found out about you when you called."

"She gave you up when she was sixteen. That's

understandable because she was so young."

"Yeah, we'll talk more at home. I need wine for this conversation."

"I completely understand."

Once settled at Missy's place, an apartment on the third story of a home, Lily made herself comfortable on an old floral sofa with a blanket thrown over the back. Missy handed her a glass of white wine.

"So tell me your story first," Missy said. "Why'd she give you up? She must've been older by then."

Lily nodded. "She was eighteen." She told her what she knew about her mom being her dad's mistress and how Lily had been bait that didn't work out.

Missy shook her head. "That doesn't surprise me at all."

"It was different with you, though. She was still in high school."

"Yes, and I don't blame her for that. I had a great adoptive family. But then they died in an accident, a car crash, when I was ten. Taylor had sent me birthday cards over the years, so I had her address. I wrote and asked her to come for me. She didn't. I ended up with an aunt, my adoptive mother's sister, who didn't really want me but needed the money from social services. She eventually married a jerk." She took a long swallow of wine and looked away. "He made a pass at me when I was fifteen."

Lily gasped.

"Yeah." Missy drained her wine and poured another glass. "I was terrified. I ran away and lived on the streets for six months. Not so bad in California. At least I never froze to death. I ended up in a series of foster homes until I married at eighteen to the first guy who promised to take care of me." She sipped her wine. "We had it good for a year, and then he decided he didn't like the way I dressed or the way I had friends at work." Her voice lowered. "He started hitting me when he was mad."

Lily felt tears leak out. "I'm so sorry."

Missy frowned. "So was he. I stayed for longer than I should. I finally made a break for it three years later. Thankfully we never had children, or I'd be tied to him forever."

Missy forced a smile. "Enough about me. Tell me all about you. I looked you up online. You're an heiress?"

Lily wasn't ready to talk about that. "But, wait, are you okay now?"

Missy nodded once. "I spent some time in counseling, so, yeah, I'm doing okay. I've got a good job as an executive assistant. And—" she smiled widely "—I just got a sister. Can't ask for more than that."

Lily blinked back tears, but this time they were

tears of joy. "I know you didn't ask for me, but now you've got family. I hope we'll stay in touch."

Missy hugged her. "Yes! You're all I've got of family. Thank you for finding me."

"You're all I've got too." Her throat got tight, and she swallowed down some wine to loosen it up. "Being an heiress sucks. My dad disowned me. Today, actually."

"Oh, honey. Your dad sounds like a real snooty asshole."

"He is! But he raised me, you know?" She fought back tears and lost, bawling her eyes out. Missy hugged her, and she battled embarrassment from crying all over this woman she'd just met and unbearable sadness over the way her dad just dumped her. Just like her mom the day she was born. Just like Nico. That set her off into fresh sobbing until her eyes felt gritty, and, finally, she had no tears left.

Lily straightened and wiped away her tears. "I'm sorry. It's been a rough day. On to more interesting topics. You want pizza?"

Missy laughed. "Pizza sounds good."

A short while later, they'd devoured half the pizza while laughing over their screwed-up families and their horrible experiences with men. Lily told her about John, and Missy told her about the string of computer geeks who asked her out at work. One of them had even serenaded her with some weird instrument called a theremin, playing her the theme to *Star Trek*.

Lily's phone vibrated, and she picked it up. A text from Nico. *You get there okay?* She replied, *I'm here. Everything's good.* He didn't reply again.

She turned to Missy. "Then there's Nico."

"Do we need more wine for this?"

Lily nodded. Missy poured them both more wine, and they settled side by side on the sofa, feet up on the coffee table. Lily told her the whole story, starting with the exciting mistaken identity kiss to their road trip, all the way to the very end when Nico seemed so set on getting one more week out of her and then saying goodbye.

"You love him," Missy said, and it wasn't a question.

She squirmed, wanting to deny it. Like admitting it would crack her heart in two. Because no one had ever loved her back.

Missy gave her a sympathetic look. "I know it's hard to say it, let alone think it. I get that. People like us—those abandoned by Taylor—are there more of us, you think?" She shook her head. "You never feel like anyone could really love you when your mom gives you up. You always think, deep down, that it must've been something wrong with you. But it wasn't! That's one thing I learned in therapy. It was never our fault, and we do deserve love."

Lily blinked and tried to let that sink in.

Missy spoke gently. "Is Nico worth it? Is he worth taking a chance on?"

She thought of Nico and how he'd treated her. He'd been so patient when he'd tried to teach her to drive the truck, even though she'd nearly gotten them killed. So gentle and tender when she'd been so inexperienced and nervous about getting naked with him. The way he'd held her purse while she'd gone shopping for hours, the way he'd gone with her skydiving just to help her...oh, who was she kidding, she'd been in love with him from the moment he bent her over his arm and kissed her the first time they'd met.

Lily swallowed hard before admitting, "He's worth it."

"Then fight for him."

She cleared her throat. "He, uh, doesn't want to get married again. And I want that."

"Men never think they want to get married." Missy elbowed her. "Until they do."

"I'm not sure if he feels the same way as I feel about him. He said the whole thing was a mistake."

Missy nodded sagely. "Let him miss you and see what happens. Same thing with your dad. Let them both appreciate you by not having you around. You can stay here for the next week and we can do…whatever sisters do."

"I'd love that! And you know what? Screw my dad. I'm tired of begging for any scrap of affection for him. He's never once said he loves me. He doesn't even hug me. I have to hug him and then he's like this." She did an impersonation of her dad, all stiff arms and lemon-sour lips.

Missy snort-laughed. "What a jerk. Speaking of…" She leaned forward and picked up her wineglass. "A toast to Taylor."

Lily picked up her wineglass and clinked it against Missy's. "The worst mother ever."

"Thank you, Taylor, you miserable excuse for a mother, for accidentally bringing your two screwed-up daughters together," Missy said.

They drank to that.

~ ~ ~

By the second day on the road home, Nico was absolutely miserable. He kept imagining Lily sitting across from him in the cab of the truck. He kept seeing that red hair, the electric blue eyes, her soft curves. Her sweet cherry scent lingered. Her voice was stuck in his head, her laughter, her tears. He had to get her out of his mind before he went insane. This closeness, this pain of letting someone into his heart was exactly what he'd avoided for years. He hadn't even felt this bad when he got his divorce. That had been a relief. This was a whole different level of pain.

He hated this feeling. He just hoped she found the happiness she deserved. The kind she could only get without him. Even if he wanted to be with her, he couldn't. Her dad had disowned her for being with him.

He called Luke at a rest stop after that second long, torturous day of driving just to get out of his own screwed-up, obsessive head.

"What's wrong?" Luke asked. "You don't sound like yourself."

"Nothing. I'm just tired. I've been driving for twelve hours straight."

"Well, get some rest. How's the heiress?"

"We broke up."

"What do you mean you broke up? I thought it was just a two-week fling."

"I got too close." His throat closed. "I gotta go. See ya Thursday night."

"Hey, Nic, take care of yourself. Don't let her get to you."

Too late, he thought miserably. "Yeah, thanks. Bye." He stared at his cell, debating calling Lily. Just to check in. He could do that as friends, right?

Except he felt pathetic. They'd been a helluva lot

more than friends. He stared at her picture on his cell. He loved this picture. It was her brave face right after he'd kissed her on the Ferris wheel.

Don't call, he told himself. And then he dialed.

She answered with a cheerful hello that was a slap in the face to his misery. He hung up.

It's over, he told himself. *She doesn't need you. Get over it.*

He'd fix this thing with her dad and move on. Lily had more than earned her place as the Spencer heiress, putting up with a lifetime of disdain and hurt. He'd make sure she got her family legacy back and quietly step out of her life forever.

CHAPTER SEVENTEEN

Nico made it to the bachelor party. He'd driven home like a madman because Lily's absence from his truck and from his bed was killing him. He kept expecting to see her or hear her when there was nothing. It had only taken him four days to drive back home as he tried to outrun his memories. He'd crashed into bed and slept fourteen hours. And then he'd been too depressed to get off the sofa. He still had to confront her father, but not yet. Everything hurt too bad. He'd end up killing the guy in a rage.

He stepped inside Lombardi's, an Italian restaurant in Eastman his family frequently went to, and headed to the reserved private room in back.

"Nico!" Vince boomed. "You made it." His brother clapped him on the back, making him feel guilty that he'd almost missed it just to hook up with Lily. Family came first. He knew that. Lily had turned his head all around.

"Of course I made it," Nico replied, forcing a smile. "Wouldn't miss the last chance to see you in your prime."

Vince barked out a laugh. "I'm in my prime, don't worry about that. Sophia keeps me on my toes."

"What'd she say about the stripper?" he asked, genuinely curious what his soon-to-be sister-in-law had to say on the matter. Sophia always spoke her mind and kept Vince in line.

"She said I could look, but not touch." Vince shook his head. "What do I need a stripper for when I've got the most beautiful woman in the world waiting for me at home? I'm going to pay the stripper a little something extra to give Angel a lap dance."

Nico laughed. Angel would be too polite to push the stripper away. He'd likely stay afterward to talk to her about an alternate profession. He couldn't help himself when it came to bettering the lives of others.

"Get yourself a beer," Vince said. "Open bar."

Nico headed over to the bar, where his stepbrothers Luke, Jared, and Gabe were all lined up. All three were in deep conversation.

"What'd I miss?" Nico asked.

Luke looked guilty. Jared and Gabe were quiet.

Jared finally broke the silence. "Beer?"

"Yeah." He gave the bartender his order and turned back to his brothers. "Were you talking about me?"

Jared elbowed him. "Nah. We'd be too bored."

Nico grabbed the beer set in front of him and took a long pull. "I'm fine."

"Luke said he stopped by your place yesterday and you wouldn't get off the sofa," Gabe said.

"I was tired," he snapped. "I'd just driven cross-country." He scowled at all three of them and turned to Gabe. "Did you look into that thing I told you about?"

"I need some kind of proof for defamation of character, not just hearsay," Gabe said. "But I'm working on it."

"Well, business sucks, so there's proof," Nico said.

"What's this now?" Jared asked.

Gabe filled him in on Lily's dad and the blackballing he'd done over Nico's shop.

Jared whistled. "That sucks. But don't worry, Gabe'll take care of ya."

Nico hung his head. That wasn't even the worst of his problems and none of his brothers could help him with the fact that he'd been stupid enough to let a woman in close enough to destroy him. His heart was in a vise and everything hurt. He'd even called her yesterday to no response. It was hopeless. They were finished.

A silence fell over the group until Luke spoke up.

"Told you guys," Luke said. "Not one smile from this guy after a week of hooking up—"

Nico grabbed Luke by the front of the shirt. Luke's dark blue eyes met his, full of sympathy. He dropped his hold on him.

Jared slung an arm around Nico's shoulders. "Hey, the stripper is a beauty. I saw her at another bachelor party. Blond, busty, just your type."

Nico shook him off and drank more beer. His type had red hair, electric blue eyes, a sprinkle of freckles across her nose. Sweet, soft curves. He let out a long, quiet breath of despair.

"He's got it bad," Luke said.

Nico scowled. "I do not have it bad."

"Just own it, man," Luke said. "If you want her, go after her."

"Who the hell are you? Some damn relationship expert?" Luke had never stayed with anyone longer than three months. Nico had been married for an entire hellish year. He knew a lot more than his brother.

"He has a relationship," Jared told Gabe.

"Sounds serious," Gabe said.

"It's not serious!" Nico exclaimed. "It was a fling, and it's over." That pissed him off so bad that he slammed his beer on the bar and headed out to the parking lot for some fresh air.

"Sure hope you catch the bouquet on Saturday!" Jared called.

Nico flipped him the bird and kept going. He stalked around the block a couple of times, realized he was being an ass on Vince's big night and headed back in.

The stripper wore sequins, which reminded Nico of Lily's mom and her showgirl act, which reminded him of how crappy Lily's family was and how she suffered because of it. Everything reminded him of Lily. Every damn thing.

He stood there staring and finally blinked, annoyed at the way his eyes stung. He looked away from the woman dancing and stripping her way toward Angel, who looked nervous. Luke caught Nico's eye and gave him a slow nod. The silent communication said he knew Nico had got in deep. It said he understood, and he'd be there for him. Luke, more than anyone, had helped him get through his divorce. He'd been more hurt over feeling like a failure, due to Ava's constant harping that he'd never amount to anything, than he'd been over the loss of Ava. This thing with Lily was so much worse.

Nico blew out a breath and inclined his head at Luke. All that from a nod. Yup. Because that was the kind of brothers they were. Tight. Family.

Lily deserved some family on her side too. He

scowled. Why did every freaking thought circle back around to Lily? She had family now. Her sister. She wasn't going to be part of his. He was never…he suddenly felt like he couldn't get enough air.

"Nico!" Vince hollered. "Grab him!"

Next thing he knew he was being hustled into a chair, dizzy and sweating profusely. His dad was there, holding the back of his hand to his forehead. "What happened, son?"

He pushed his dad's hand away. His brothers and some of Vince's friends were gathered around, staring at him. "I'm fine."

"Is he sick?" Angel asked.

"You better not be sick," Vince said, handing him a napkin with ice in it. "You're my best man."

Nico straightened up, pressing the cold compress to his forehead as the sweat evaporated to a cold clamminess. "I'm fine. I'm just tired from the trip."

"I'll take you home," his dad said. "You need to rest. Allie will take care of you."

"Dad, I'm fine."

Luke whispered something to his dad, who raised a brow. "Can you walk?" his dad asked.

"I'm not going anywhere," Nico said. "I'm having fun here. It's Vince's night."

"Get lost," Vince said, giving him a light slap upside the head. "You're bringing the party down with all your collapsing into chairs. I'll see you tomorrow at the rehearsal dinner. Okay? Let Ma take care of ya."

He would've argued more, but strong arms were gathered around him—Vince, Luke, Jared, his dad— lifting him and pushing him along. He headed out the door, resolved to let his stepmom give him the loving treatment. He was just far gone enough to really need it.

~ ~ ~

"Invite her for dinner," his stepmom demanded as she pushed him onto the sofa in the living room of his parents' house and covered him with a flowery blanket.

"It's over," he said, rolling to his side away from her, wanting nothing more than to drift off to sleep wedged into the sofa he'd grown up lounging on with his brothers. It was comfort, nostalgia—

"Ow!" he exclaimed.

She'd jabbed him in the back, and he turned to face her. "What was that for?"

"Nico Marino, you listen up good. Now I know that Ava did a number on you, but I refuse to watch you suffer now because of it. That was ten years ago. Luke says you're in love with Lily and that means you go after her. I want to meet her. I want you both to eat the wedding cookies—"

"I'm not eating damn wedding cookies!"

She held up a warning finger. "You know it worked for Vince."

He groaned and scrubbed a hand over his face. "I thought I was getting the loving treatment."

"This is the loving treatment! You give yourself a chance to love again. You give her a chance!"

"Her dad disowned her because of me. I'm no good for her. I'm a nobody. She's supposed to be with someone at her level."

"You're above their level if that's how their family treats each other. I'm calling her dad."

"No! I'm going to talk to him. I'll fix it. Just not now. I'm exhausted."

She studied him for a moment and brushed a hand through his hair, which did a lot to temper his annoyance with her butting into his life. "Nico," she said gently, "I hate to see you like this. You deserve some happiness."

He got choked up. "I'm just tired."

"Get some rest. Then you fix this ridiculous thing with her father and then you bring her to dinner. You hear me?" She tucked the blanket around his shoulders. "Don't make me get involved. You know I will, and then heads will roll."

For her diminutive size, his stepmom had a spine of steel. She'd kept him and his brothers in line with a firm no-nonsense attitude and an always open heart.

"She's not answering her cell," he said quietly. "I don't even know if she's back from Seattle."

"She has to come home eventually. Now get some sleep."

She left and turned out the light. He rolled over, still a little annoyed with the way she insisted he give Lily a chance, even when he knew she could destroy him. But a calm came over him for the first time since he'd left Lily back in L.A.

The next thing he knew he was out cold.

~ ~ ~

Lily hugged her sister goodbye on Saturday while a cab waited out front for her. It had been a great week doing all sorts of touristy things in Seattle, but, more importantly, just spending time together, talking until late into the night. Though they'd just met, she and Missy connected like they'd been lifelong friends. But now it was time to get back to reality. Time to face her dad.

And Nico.

Unfinished business all around.

"Do you think my dad missed me?" Lily asked. Missy was a straight shooter and didn't sugarcoat things at all.

"I know Nico did," Missy replied.

Nico had left a voicemail message wishing her well in her new job and saying he hoped they could be friends. But she hadn't replied because she didn't know what to say to that. She wasn't sure they could be friends after that crazy week together.

"Come visit me in New York," Lily said. "I'll send you a plane ticket."

"I will. I just need to get the time off work. I used a week on this visit and have to earn some more time."

"Okay. Maybe for the holidays when everyone has time off."

The cabbie honked his horn. She was going to miss her flight if she didn't leave soon.

"Definitely, then," Missy said, hugging her one last time. "Bye, little sis."

"Bye, big sis!" She rushed out the door and called over her shoulder, "I love you!"

"Love you too!"

She nearly lost her footing. It was the first time an "I love you" was returned for Lily. Her father never returned her *I love yous*. Her ex had avoided them. She headed back home, warmed by the fact that she'd finally found her loving family.

~ ~ ~

Nico stood in a tux at the front of St. Joseph's Catholic church in Clover Park on Saturday alongside the other four best men, his brothers, waiting for the bride to make an appearance. He'd placed several calls to Lily's dad at home over the last couple of days, none of which had been returned. Face to face was how it had to be, and he just hoped he could keep himself from strangling the man with his bare hands.

He glanced at Vince standing next to him at the altar, and saw not nerves, but a completely calm, almost gleeful expression. The wedding march began, and Sophia started down the aisle on the arm of her father, his own father's former archenemy, in what looked like a fancy ball gown. A strapless lacy top part fit her like a glove and poofed at the hips into layers of gown with a long train. A thin veil covered her face and trailed down her back. She looked radiantly happy. He turned back to Vince, who was dabbing at his eyes with a handkerchief, a move that normally would've invited a well-placed elbow to the ribs, but instead got Nico all choked up. Dammit. He missed Lily.

Sophia reached Vince's side and they turned as one to Father Munson. Nico caught his dad's eye sitting in the front row, holding hands with his stepmom, and his dad winked with a smile. Nico gave him a small smile back, relieved not only to see his dad back to his usual cheerful self, but also that he'd come to terms with his son marrying the daughter of his enemy. His dad had informed them all at the rehearsal dinner last night that he was thrilled with the marriage, as long as her dad stayed with his alpacas. Apparently, Sophia's dad owned an alpaca farm in Virginia. A lot of good-natured ribbing between the two dads had gone back and forth, but it seemed their feud, begun years ago over Nico's mother, was forgiven.

As the ceremony went on, Nico couldn't help remembering his own wedding to Ava. They'd gotten together after meeting at a bar when they'd both been twenty-one. She was beautiful and ambitious. He hadn't realized how ambitious until they married and she'd begun harping on him to move up from being a "greasy" mechanic to a manager. At twenty-one that hadn't been possible. He'd even talked to his boss about a timetable for eventually moving up, and Kevin had told him they'd have to wait and see. That was fine with Nico. He knew he had a lot to learn, and Kevin was the best mechanic on classic cars in the state. He was thrilled to work closely with him on expensive cars that not everyone got a chance to get their hands on. But Ava hadn't seen it that way. She'd seen it as a failing that he was content. She'd constantly pushed him to do more, complained about their small apartment, told him how sick she was of working at the salon. Her favorite refrain was "it's up to you to make me a lady of luxury." He'd promised her he would, but it would take time.

Ava wasn't the patient sort. She walked out on him a year later, pregnant and screaming that it was a more successful man's child. He'd demanded a paternity test as soon as the baby was born. It wasn't his.

His mind jerked back to the present as a cheer went up for the happy couple. His six-month-old nephew, Miles, let out a wail at the startling noise from the crowd. His sister-in-law, Zoe, comforted him as Gabe looked on anxiously from where he stood in line with his brothers. Zoe held up her hand and smiled reassuringly in a silent communication that had Gabe settling down.

Vince and Sophia rushed down the aisle, hand in hand. A pang of envy went through him. They looked so damn happy.

By the time Nico got to the reception, he was on edge. He worked his way grimly through the motions of greeting family members and friends in attendance. He danced with a bridesmaid whose name he couldn't even remember because all he could think about was when he'd crashed that wedding with Lily back in Cleveland. Visions of Lily and her crazy dancing kept running through his head. Her abandon, her lush body wiggling, and then holding her close for that slow dance just before they'd been caught and had to leave.

What was he doing begrudging his brother's happiness? He had to grab a hold of his own before he lost her forever.

He left the reception at a run because when you suddenly realize you want something lasting with someone, you have to be with them as soon as possible. He drove like a maniac to her father's house, determined to both make the man take Lily back and also hoping she was there to see him come to the rescue. Maybe she hadn't yet moved to the city. Maybe she'd consider more than a fling.

Her dad answered the door, stone-faced. "Can I help you?"

Suddenly all he wanted was Lily. "Is Lily home?"

"No."

"Where is she?"

"Why?"

"I need to see her."

George Spencer crossed his arms and looked down his nose at him. "Why?"

"Because I love her." He really did, and it took being envious of Vince's happiness as he got married to really hit home that a wedding could be in his future.

"I disowned her, so move along."

"Yeah, that was not right. You'd better re-own her or whatever it's called. You can't turn your back on your only daughter!" His hands formed fists. "Do you have any idea the pain you caused her?"

"And if I don't? Would you still want her if she had nothing?"

"Of course I do!"

George raised his brows. "You passed the test."

Nico bristled. "What test?"

"Will you sign a prenup?"

"What test?" he repeated.

George uncrossed his arms. "Come in."

Nico stepped inside a two-story foyer with marble flooring, columns, and a huge crystal chandelier overhead.

George went on. "I wanted to see if you had no business, no money, and no chance at Lily's money, if you'd still want her. That's why I disowned her."

"You bastard!" He hauled back his fist and just before he could land a right hook a voice cried out.

"Nico!"

He turned to see Lily standing in the foyer, with a look of utter shock on her face. A pink-shirted, blond, twenty-something guy that reeked of money and husband material stood at her side.

He stalked toward her. "Who the hell is this?"

"I'm Trevor," the man replied stiffly. Trevor was a couple inches shorter than Nico. He could take him. "And who are you?"

"Nico, what are you doing here?" Lily asked. "And why are you wearing a tux?"

"I'm making sure your dad doesn't disown you!"

"That's why we're here," Trevor said, puffing out his chest. Like *he* was the damn knight in shining armor.

"Trevor!" Nico hollered. "Get the hell out of here!" He turned to Lily. "One week after you're in my bed and you're hooking up with the man Daddy wants you to marry? What the hell?"

Trevor shoved him. "How dare you talk about Lily like that." He cocked a fist. "Why, I ought to—"

Nico let loose with a right hook that landed perfectly, knocking Trevor right off his feet. Though it would've been more satisfying if it had been her dad.

"Nico!" Lily cried, rushing to Trevor's side.

"Is this the kind of man you want, Lily?" her dad asked.

"You're talking to me again?" Lily asked her dad.

"I'm calling the police," her dad said.

"I still want to marry you, Lily," Trevor said weakly from the floor.

Nico grabbed her hand and pulled her out the door.

CHAPTER EIGHTEEN

"What the hell, Nico!" Lily shouted. "You can't just show up at my dad's house and beat up on people."

Nico shoved a hand in his hair. "I meant to punch your dad, but then Trevor was there. He put his hands on me first!"

"Nico." She shook her head. "Why are you here?"

"Because I needed to fix things. I told your dad he can't disown you."

She pressed both hands to her temples. "I can't deal with this right now. I just flew in, and I've been working up to confronting my dad."

He jabbed a hand in the air. "So you went to Trevor for backup? Why didn't you call me?"

"I thought you were at your brother's wedding. You are!" She suddenly realized what the tux meant. "Go back!" She shoved at him, but he didn't move.

"It's just the reception. I'm not going anywhere."

They had a standoff. Nico glared at her, and she

glared right back.

And then a cop pulled up, lights flashing. "Go!" Lily urged.

He crossed his arms. The officer approached them.

"Officer," Nico said with a nod.

"We got a call of a domestic disturbance," the officer said.

"Inside," Lily said.

The officer went inside. As soon as the door shut behind him, Lily gave Nico a shove and met hard muscle. "Get out of here and don't come back! My dad will have a restraining order on you by the time this is done."

"I want a chance," he said, stubbornly not leaving. "For us."

"I can't be with someone who uses their fists before words," she said, which was true, but she said it mostly to keep him out of trouble with the police. He had to leave right away. But the look of despair that crossed his features made her waver. "I mean—"

"I understand," he said quietly. He turned and left.

"Wait!" she called, but he kept going.

And then she was being summoned by her dad and the police. And she had to clear Nico's name and beg Trevor not to press charges. He agreed if Lily would consider his proposal one more time. Which she promised she would, even if she already knew the answer would be no. And then, finally, it was just her and her dad left at home. Wherever he'd gone. He'd left her and Trevor to hash things out in privacy.

She headed back to the conservatory, where he often liked to relax. She'd had some time to think about things while she stayed at her sister's place. And as she'd heard more about Missy's life after her adoptive parents died, she'd realized that what she'd had growing up with her tough-love dad maybe wasn't the worst thing ever. He'd taught her the value of hard work and forging ahead even when things seemed awful. She could've been raised by the selfish Taylor, after all.

She found him sitting in his favorite chair, smoking his pipe and reading *The New York Times* like it was just another Saturday night.

"I refuse to accept you disowning me," she announced. "I'm your daughter and nothing will ever change that."

He dropped the paper. "About damn time you came home."

"So I'm not disowned anymore? You're speaking to me?"

"That was just a test to see if Nico wanted you with no Spencer money."

She nearly keeled over in shock. "Are you kidding me? Do you know how devastated I was?"

His brows drew together. "Why would you be devastated? You still had your trust fund." He looked genuinely puzzled.

"Because we're family," she said, not bothering to hide her irritation.

"I know we're family."

"Well, you don't disown family! Especially when you only have one kid!"

"I told you it was a test."

She threw her hands up. "Now you tell me! You might've let me in on it."

"Well, then it wouldn't have worked. You'd probably tell Nico, and we'd never know." He returned to his paper. "Now we know."

"What do we know, Dad? What did *we* learn?"

He peered at her over the paper. "We learned he's low class. I mean, really. Fists?"

"He fought for me, which is more than you ever did."

He went back to his paper and all the years of feeling ignored, of begging for one scrap of affection poured through her in an overwhelming wave of pure white-hot rage. She grabbed the paper and ripped it in two.

"Lily! What's come over you? Is this Nico's influence?"

"Nico treated me better than anyone ever has. And

you know what? I disown you."

His brows drew together. "You can't disown me. It doesn't work that way."

"I'm done with begging for scraps of affection or your time. I'm tired of being nothing but an annoyance for you. I deserve better than that."

"Like that low-class greasy mechanic?"

She threw the newspaper shreds in the air. "I'd be lucky to have him!"

She turned and left, wanting nothing more than to see Nico. She had to apologize, had to let him know she wanted to give them a chance too.

She got to her car and realized she didn't know where the wedding reception was. She didn't even know where he lived. She called him and it went to voicemail. She texted him instead. *I'm sorry.*

His reply was devastatingly short. *Don't be. You deserve Trevor.*

It felt like a slap. Was this the life she deserved? A society life? A society marriage? A heartless, soulless existence?

I love you, she texted. Her finger hovered over the send button.

She deleted it.

~ ~ ~

Nico returned to his apartment after the wedding

reception completely exhausted and defeated. He'd done his best, standing up to Lily's dad, asking Lily to give them a chance. Yet he'd shown her the kind of man he really was. The kind who used his fists. He'd never be that country club kind of guy she was used to. The kind of person she was, really, deep down.

He stopped short. Lily was sitting on the bottom step of the long wooden staircase that led to his studio apartment.

"You drive a Porsche, yet you live above someone's garage?" she asked.

"How did you find me?"

"I looked you up online, but you're tough to find because you rent and you only use your cell. So I called one of the other Marinos in Eastman. Your stepmom gave me your address."

Figured. "Why're you here?"

She stood. "Can I come in?"

"I thought you were mad at me."

"Please."

He shook his head. "C'mon." He climbed the stairs and opened the door to his apartment, holding it to let her in. He took in the small space of his apartment, all one room with a small kitchenette. The bathroom was separate. The walls were white and empty of any decoration. The floor had cheap beige carpet. It was a far cry from what Lily was used to.

"I know it's not much," he said. "I've been saving all my money to buy out Kevin. And I drive a Porsche because I can't run a business restoring and selling classic cars while driving some piece-of-shit car."

She looked around. "Where do you sleep?"

"The sofa pulls out."

She just stood there, quiet and subdued. He figured she was probably sorry she showed up here.

He took off the tux jacket and threw it over the arm of the sofa. "Look, I told you I had nothing to offer you." He undid the bow tie and cummerbund and tossed them with the jacket. "I'm just a grease monkey who uses his fists." He went to the small refrigerator and pulled off the check he'd stuck there under a magnet.

"It's the full hundred grand," he said, handing it to her. "I earn my own way."

She tucked it into her purse without a word. He could just imagine what she was thinking. That he wasn't a success. That this wasn't the kind of life she'd ever want.

"I like my life," he told her. "I never asked for more. I never wanted more." Until you, he added silently.

She looked at him with those electric blues, and he read pain in those eyes.

"Lily, why're you here?"

She finally spoke. "I didn't love that you hurt Trevor, but I loved that you cared enough to fight for me." She swallowed. "I love you," she said in a soft voice.

He couldn't quite believe what he was hearing. "What?"

She pressed her lips into a flat line and blinked rapidly. "Please don't make me say it again. I've had a rough day. A rough week. A rough li—"

He hauled her close and kissed her as pure relief coursed through him. He pulled back to look in her eyes. "I love you too." He crushed her to him. "I missed you so much."

"I missed you too." She wrapped her arms tight around him, and they just held each other. "Can I stay here for a while?" she whispered. "I'm sort of homeless for a few weeks. I disowned my dad and my apartment's not ready until July first."

He pulled away in shock. "You disowned your dad?"

"Yes," she said as she peeled off her shirt. "It's been a rough night and I just want to be with you."

He blinked as she stripped down in record time. A naked Lily made it hard to think, but something was off.

She looked at him. "Why aren't you getting naked?"

He unbuttoned the top two buttons of his dress shirt. "Are you okay?"

Her lower lip trembled. He pulled her in close and stroked her back. "Hey, it'll be okay."

She broke down in tears, and he just held her until she was done. He knew something was off. He'd be extra tender with her tonight.

"Be right back," he told her. He grabbed a condom from the bathroom, stuck it in his pocket and when he returned to her, she started kissing and biting his neck hard enough to sting, which triggered a primal aggressive side he tried to keep in check. The last time he'd been with her he'd been too rough, taking her against the wall. She'd probably had bruises on her back from the way he pounded against her.

He took over the kiss, sliding his hand into her hair, slowing things down.

She bit his lip. Hard.

He held her by the shoulders a distance away. "You're getting me revved up," he warned, "and I don't want to be like I was last time."

She slipped out from under his grip, leaned her hot curvy body against him, and squeezed his ass with both hands. "How were you last time?"

His hand came up to her throat, and she threw her head back. "Rough," he growled as his fingers stroked down her throat. "You deserve tenderness. Especially after what happened with—"

She kissed him aggressively just as her hand shot out straight to his cock. "Fuck me," she demanded.

That thin line of control broke. His mouth slammed into hers, his tongue thrust deep, his hands stroked her ass as he wedged his leg between hers. Her hands were all over him and her hips rocked against him, stealing all rational thought. He had to have her. He maneuvered her to the wall and pressed his body fully against her soft curves. She gasped, and he remembered her back. He grabbed her and turned her, bending her over and placing her palms against the wall. He couldn't wait even long enough to strip down, just freed himself, rolled on the condom, and entwined his fingers with hers, pinning her hands against the wall.

"Nico," she sighed.

His name on her lips was the sweetest invitation. And then she lifted her hips, arching back, demanding he take, and with one fierce thrust he took her.

"Yes," she hissed out on a long breath.

Nothing had ever felt so right. Her body was hot and tight, clenching around him as he took fiercely, no holding back, and she gave. He wasn't going to last long. He reached around, slid his fingers between her slick folds, stroking quickly until she cried out, milking him with her release. He grabbed her hips and yanked her back hard against him as he drove deep. She got noisy then, which only spurred him on as he took those final deep thrusts into oblivion. He came with a roar and pumped until he had nothing left, dimly aware she was now moaning softly. He loosened his grip on her hips and stayed like that for a moment, buried deep within her, catching his breath. He pulled out. She sank to her knees, resting her forehead against the wall.

He dropped to his knees and wrapped his arms around her from behind. He worried he'd been too rough, but he couldn't speak yet to apologize.

"Nico," she said hoarsely.

He tightened his hold on her. "I'll be gentler next time."

She lifted her head and said over her shoulder, "You can take me any way you like." She turned in his arms. The pain was gone from her eyes. She was flushed pink, eyes shining. "I'm yours."

She held his gaze, those electric blue eyes reflecting pure acceptance of her place with him.

He pressed his thumb to her plump lower lip in his own primal claim. "You're mine."

And with those two simple words, he knew he'd never be able to let her go.

CHAPTER NINETEEN

The nightmares were back. Lily hadn't had this dream in years. She was being put out in the pile of stuff to be donated to charity, but no one noticed her in the pile of toys and clothes and old appliances. "Don't throw me away!" she yelled until she was hoarse.

But she always got tossed with the rest of the stuff as her dad walked away. She woke with a start, eyes wide, heart pounding.

"Hey." Nico pulled her into his arms and stroked her back. "Just a dream."

"Sorry," she mumbled. "Didn't mean to wake you. I haven't had that dream in a long time."

She curled into his chest. He was quiet. Maybe he fell back asleep. "I used to have that dream every night for a year when I was ten. I'm being tossed with the pile of unwanted stuff."

He was still quiet, so she went on. "I know why. My dad donated the Kaitlyn doll I used to sleep with every night because he decided I was too old for it. I saw it being taken away in this pile of stuff, and he wouldn't let me get it. I guess I always wondered when I would be next."

She rested her ear right over his heart, eyes wide open, hoping listening to that steady thump would keep her from falling back into the dream. Once the dream had a hold of her, she could have it multiple times a night.

Her eyes gradually closed, trapping her in the nightmare once more. She was running from a giant dump truck scoop. "Don't throw me away!" She was running and running and running and not getting anywhere. Then she was scooped and dumped back in the pile of unwanted items, screaming to not be thrown away until she was hoarse.

When she woke again, very late on Sunday morning, it was to the delicious scent of coffee. Nico was standing, already dressed in T-shirt and jeans, leaning against the counter in the small kitchen, sipping his coffee.

She sat up. "I hope I didn't keep you up last night."

He gazed at her for a long moment, and then he set his coffee down and crossed to her, pulling something out of his pocket. He sat on the bed next to her, took her hand, and placed the object in her hand, wrapping her fingers around it.

"I'm keeping you, Lil. You're worth keeping."

Her breath caught as she realized he must've heard her middle-of-the-night confession. She opened her hand to find a small turquoise ring.

"It was my mother's," he said.

Her heart stuttered at the shocking gift he was giving her, that apparently he hadn't given to his first wife. She knew his mom had died when he was just a kid. The value of the ring to him and his family made her feel like it was the most precious gift in the world.

"Nico," she choked out. "I don't know what to say."

"You don't have to say anything." He tried to slide the ring on her ring finger, but it was too small. She laughed, a hiccupping laugh, and slid it on her pinky finger.

"Thank you," she said, staring at the ring through a haze of unshed tears.

"I'm taking you to meet my family for Sunday dinner tonight," he said.

Her throat got tight. "I'd like that very much."

He gave her a quick kiss and went back to the kitchen, pouring some coffee in a second mug. She slipped on her shirt from the day before and joined him.

"This feels like a good day to start my life as the

new Lily," she said.

He handed her the mug of coffee. "Yeah? What's that mean?"

"It means I'm done feeling bad that my dad never said he loved me—" Nico tensed, and she put her hand on his arm. "Some people just aren't capable of love. I'm done sending my mother money, hoping she might one day love me."

He took her mug, set it on the counter, and pulled her close.

"You made it all possible," she said. "It all started with your sex tutorial."

He pulled back. "My what?"

"That's why I wanted you at first." She felt herself flush. "Because I was so inexperienced. I thought it would help me be the more confident, experienced Lily."

A small smile played over his lips. "You sure made me work for it, considering that was the plan."

"I know. I didn't anticipate how crazy nervous I'd get when faced with an Italian underwear model."

He barked out a laugh. "All right. I'll take that."

She met his dark brown eyes. "But you showed me so much more. So much kindness, so much tenderness." A tear leaked out and then another. "And now this ring."

"It's not a proposal."

She nodded through her tears. "I know. I never thought—"

"It's too soon for that." He brushed her tears from her cheeks with his thumbs and then cradled her face in his large hands. "I just want you to know that I want that now." His eyes reflected such tenderness that it felt like her heart would burst. "Marriage, I mean, if I can have it with you...down the road."

"Yes," she choked out.

He nodded once, and then he stepped back and pulled off his T-shirt with that masculine two-handed move he did. She wiped her tears to watch.

"You ready for your Italian underwear model?" he asked just as he pulled down the jeans.

She leaped at him.

~ ~ ~

Lily felt the love the minute she stepped into Nico's parents' cozy home and understood immediately where his innate warmth and touchy-feely nature came from.

A petite blond woman answered the door and looked surprised to see her.

"I brought her," Nico said, like the woman already knew about her.

"Hello, I'm Allie, Nico's stepmom," the woman said, enveloping Lily in a big hug. "So nice to meet you. If I'd known you were coming, I would've made something special." She shot Nico a look and then ushered them both inside.

An older Italian man stood and greeted them in the living room. Same dark hair, dark eyes, and olive skin as Nico. He took her hand in his and held it warmly. "A pleasure to meet you. I'm Vinny, Nico's dad."

"Nice to meet you," she said. "I'm Lily."

Another gorgeous guy pushed off the sofa. Tall, muscular, short dirty blond hair, green eyes, and a smile that made a dimple appear in his right cheek. She didn't think she'd ever get used to how cute Nico's brothers were. Not as gorgeous as Nico, but still...wow. The man shook her hand in a firm grip. "I'm Jared. And you must be the redhead who slapped him."

Her cheeks burned. She didn't know Nico had told his whole family about that.

"One of them," Nico said, rubbing his stubbled cheek. "Two slaps from two redheads that day."

"There was a mix-up," Lily rushed to explain. She didn't want his parents to think she went around slapping their son all the time.

Jared leaned close and grinned. "He had it coming, didn't he?"

"Yes and no," she said.

Jared raised his brows. "What'd he do?"

Nico's parents looked at them with interest. She wasn't about to—ah! Nico dipped her over his arm. Then he gave her a quick kiss and pulled her back upright.

She smoothed her hair. "So…"

Jared socked Nico on the arm. "Smooth."

Nico pulled her in close and kissed her hair. His stepmom beamed at them.

Nico's older stepbrother, Gabe, arrived then with his wife, Zoe, and their adorable baby, Miles, who everyone fussed over. Lily was happy to have the attention shift to the baby, still getting used to Nico's easy affection, especially in front of other people.

Gabe wasn't as tall as his brothers, Jared and Luke, but he had the same good looks with light brown hair and dark blue eyes. His wife, Zoe, was a bundle of warm energy, her bright brown eyes lighting up as she greeted each of them in turn. Finally, it was Lily's turn to be introduced.

"I am so excited to meet Nico's girlfriend!" Zoe exclaimed. "You're the first woman he's brought home in ten years! You must be very special to him."

Lily was tongue-tied. "Thank you," she managed.

Nico wrapped his arm around her. "She is."

"Aww!" Zoe exclaimed. "Lily, you want to help out in the kitchen with me and Vinny? We'll let you in on the secret ravioli recipe."

"Ooh, secret family recipes," Lily said. "I must've hit the jackpot."

"She did, actually," Nico said. "The only person I know to win at roulette. Twelve large."

"You're kidding!" Zoe exclaimed. "That's amazing! And p.s. I want to hear all about your trip."

Lily joined them in the kitchen, happy to be cooking again.

Mr. Marino shook his head. "Lily, if I show you the recipe, you have to promise to come back and make it with me."

"I promise," she said.

"And you can't share it with anyone," Zoe said. "Family rules."

Lily nodded. "Absolutely."

A man with tousled dark brown hair and a dimpled smile poked his head in the kitchen. "Hey, what's this I hear? Sharing family secrets?"

"Angel, when're you going to bring Julia by?" Mr. Marino asked.

"She's busy," Angel said before turning to Lily. "You must be Lily." He crossed to her and shook her hand. "Luke told us about you. Said you had Nico good, and you're here, so he must've been right."

She flushed. "Nice to meet you, Angel."

"How's Nico treating you?" Angel asked.

"How you think?" Nico barked, appearing out of nowhere and making Angel jump.

"Nico." Angel gave him a one-armed man hug. "Good to see you. How you feeling?"

Nico ruffled his hair and gave his head a little shove. "Fine."

"Was something wrong?" Lily asked.

Angel exchanged a look with Mr. Marino and the men were quiet.

"Were you sick?" Lily asked Nico.

"Nah. Just tired from driving. I wasn't feeling well at Vince's bachelor party. I'm fine now."

"Oh."

"I'll bet Vince and Sophia are having a blast in Mexico," Zoe said. "Gabe and I never had a honeymoon on account of Miles."

"That's what happens when you get knocked up, Z," Luke said as he stepped into the kitchen.

Zoe laughed and Luke swooped in to give her a warm hug. Luke turned to Lily. "Got you at the family dinner, huh? You must be in."

"In what?" Lily asked.

Luke blew Nico a kiss. "In love."

"Shut up," Nico said, but he sounded happy. "Why don't you shave your beard, you damn hipster."

Luke scratched at his beard. "I'm going for the boss look. Hope to be soon." He turned to Lily. "You in love too?"

Lily glanced at Nico, who gazed back warmly; then she looked around the room at all the expectant faces. She beamed. "I am. He gave me this ring." She held out her hand to show off his mom's turquoise ring.

"Nico," his dad said quietly.

Nico gave him a quick nod. There was an exchange of looks around the room. Zoe grabbed her hand. "C'mon, let's get that pasta maker cranking!"

Dinner was happy chaos. A far cry from the formal dinners she shared with her father, both of them sitting at opposite ends of the long cherrywood table from each other as her father insisted. The only sound the clink of silverware. Nico's family crowded around an oak table with two leaves set in place. A high chair was set a short distance away for Miles.

His stepmom asked each of them in turn what was new and followed up with things she remembered that were going on in their lives. Zoe apparently was a jazz singer and about to put out her first solo album. Luke was up for a promotion at work. Angel was a school social worker and planned to spend the summer working at a camp for kids with special needs. Lily was content to sit back and listen until Mrs. Marino got to her.

"Tell us about your new job, Lily," Mrs. Marino said. "I heard you're a lawyer like our Gabe."

"Don't practice small-town law," Gabe said. "I used to in Clover Park. They cornered the market on the ridiculous. I ended up mediating arguments over an old man who gets his mail in his boxers."

Everyone laughed.

"I'm working at the Earth Defense Group in the city," she said. "I start after the fourth of July. Bar exam's at the end of July. Nico helped me study—" she grinned at him "—involuntarily on our road trip."

Nico groaned. "She had these awful audio lectures—"

"And he refused to quiz me with flash cards," she put in.

Nico made a crazy gesture, circling his temple with his finger. "Eight *hundred* flash cards. But I did take her skydiving."

"He barfed," she said. His brothers roared with laughter.

"She passed out," Nico hollered over the laughter.

"Sounds like the perfect couple," Mrs. Marino said. And darn if not every single one of them pinned her with a warm smile. Nico took her hand and squeezed it.

Lily had never felt so loved.

CHAPTER TWENTY

Business was booming. Nico didn't know what to make of it at first. New clients called or showed up every day, saying George Spencer sent them. The auction for Lily's Mustang in two weeks promised to have record attendance. Part of that was the car. Within a few days, he'd fixed the brakes and gotten it running. It was in remarkably good shape from being stored in the dry California air. He'd called the press and the car world was buzzing with the story. Word had spread fast about the untouched beauty, practically a museum relic. Still, he had to wonder if Lily's dad was helping spread the word too. The attention on the car, his shop, and the auction was bigger than anything he'd seen in sixteen years of living and breathing the car world. It was, he suspected, George's weird way of helping Lily by helping him. Just like he'd hurt Nico to hurt Lily. Twisted bastard.

Nico had never paid Lily anything for the car, so he planned on giving her the proceeds for the full amount. He didn't want her money. So what if he had to work harder before he became full owner of the shop? He didn't deserve to be a success just by taking what she gave him. He had to earn it. He'd always known that.

Lily hadn't been quite herself since cutting off her dad, and it pained him to see her suffer. She tossed and turned at night, still having that nightmare that had her screaming not to throw her away every night, though once he woke her and soothed her she settled back into a quiet sleep. She studied for the bar exam while he was at work, and when he got home, though she was happy to see him, he could tell she was still struggling with the way things had gone down with her dad. It wasn't anything she said. It was just a bone-deep weariness about her. A smile that didn't quite reach her eyes. It was subtle, but he'd spent a week on the road tuned in to her every movement, every tone, every sigh, and he knew she wasn't happy.

So when the auction finally rolled around with the man himself in attendance, Nico took the opportunity to confront Lily's dad before the bidding began. Lily had stayed home, not wanting to see her dad.

"Hello, George," Nico said, cornering the man where he stood in the back of the large car auction room in a luxury hotel. A stage was set at one end with the Mustang on display. Several other classic cars would also be auctioned today, but the Mustang was the star of the show and had been brought out in a preshow display to build excitement in the bidding.

George looked down his nose at him. "Looks like Lily will see a nice profit on the auction. I'll put my own name in the ring."

Nico fought the urge to yell at the man who had no clue just how much he was hurting his own daughter. "I appreciate the attendance here and all my new clients. I know you had something to do with that."

George's lips puckered. "Well deserved."

"Thank you. But, you know, I'm still disappointed."

George's brows shot up. "How could you be disappointed with all this?" He gestured around to the crowd of several hundred people milling about and the long line waiting to inspect the car.

"You're helping me to help Lily, I figure. But all she wants is to know that you love her. You know her mom is shit. Her stepmom resents her." He got in George's face, eye to eye. "Be a man. Tell your daughter you love her."

George took a step back. "How dare you speak to me that way! Who the hell do you think you are?"

"I'm the man who's going to marry her."

George stared at him for a long moment, probably trying to decide if he measured up. "Will you sign a prenup?"

Nico shook his head, beyond frustrated. "Not everything is about money. I'll do whatever Lily wants. There's nothing I care about more than her happiness. And if that means I have to deal with *you*, then that's what I'll do." He jabbed a finger in George's chest. "*Man up.*"

George hissed out a breath. "I'm more of a man than you'll ever be."

Nico cocked his head. "Yeah? Prove it."

George sputtered and then walked stiffly away.

~ ~ ~

Nico left the hotel after a very long day at the auction and headed out to the parking lot. Lily's car sold for even more than he'd predicted. Seven hundred grand from a last-minute over-the-phone bid. Even outbid old George Spencer. Ha!

Someone was standing next to his Porsche. A country-club type. He got closer and saw his front tire was slashed. Dammit. Those were expensive tires. He spared no expense when it came to his car. It was a 1971 Porsche 911 E. His baby. His first classic car that he'd bought with his own hard-earned cash. He picked up speed and recognized Trevor, the guy who wanted to marry Lily.

"You fucking kidding me with this!" Nico hollered. "You're going to pay to replace that tire." He did a quick circle around the car to check on the other tires, careful not to turn his back to Trevor. It was just the one tire.

Trevor veered unsteadily toward him. He reeked of alcohol. Great. And then a glint of light reflecting off metal caught his eye. Trevor was gripping a switchblade.

Nico took a step back. "We're even. I punched you. You destroyed my tire. Put the knife down."

Trevor brandished the knife high in the air, and Nico felt a moment of panic because Trevor looked just psycho enough to use it. Nico knew he could take him without the knife, but with, he could get sliced. The man was nearly his size.

Nico took a careful step back. "I get it. You want to marry Lily."

Trevor sneered and the knife came down, still pointing right at Nico. "Her dad promised to sponsor my bid for governor if I married the bitch." Spittle formed on his lips. "And you ruined everything!"

"So find another heiress to marry," Nico said.

"There aren't any with her kind of money in Connecticut. We're a dying breed!" Trevor sliced with the knife close to Nico's arm, and he dodged it.

"What's the game plan here?" Nico said. "Going to knife me in the hotel parking lot in broad daylight? You think no one will notice a bloody body here?"

Trevor brandished the knife unsteadily. "Lily told me once and for all no tonight." Rage poured through Nico. Had Trevor confronted Lily like this? Did he threaten her too?

Nico stopped backing up and started edging closer.

"She says she's in love with you," Trevor said, waving the knife around. "So I'm asking you to walk away before things get ugly."

"They already have. Go for it." He held his palms up. "I got a right hook in. Go ahead and take your best shot."

Trevor lunged with the knife, losing his balance as he just managed to graze Nico's arm with a small cut. Nico jabbed his elbow into Trevor's nose, grabbed the wrist holding the knife, and squeezed until Trevor dropped the knife. Nico kicked it away. Then he hauled Trevor up by the collar of his designer polo shirt and shook him. "Did you see Lily tonight? Did you threaten her?"

"N-no. She told me no over the phone."

His rage simmered down a notch. "I better not see you ever again. And if you go anywhere near Lily, you will find yourself in hell. And I'll be the one driving you there. I've got five brothers my size to back me up. How you like those odds?"

"She'll never be happy with you," Trevor spat. "She's got a lifestyle."

Nico shook him again. "I'm gonna keep this real simple for that little hamster-wheel brain. Get out of here before I kick your ass." He tossed him to the pavement. Trevor glared at him from the ground, but made no move to get up.

Just to show Trevor how much of a non-threat he considered him, Nico went about getting the spare tire from the trunk. Trevor was still lying on the ground, holding his wrist.

Nico lifted out the spare tire. He stopped next to the slashed tire, set the spare down, and lurched suddenly toward Trevor. "Get lost!"

Trevor took off at a run.

~ ~ ~

Lily turned down Trevor. For the last time. She was very firm and told him her answer was final. The whole thing happened over the phone while Nico was at the auction. She'd finally returned Trevor's call after he'd left twenty increasingly pathetic messages. She'd never loved him.

When Nico had told her about the auction and that her dad would be bidding, she immediately knew she wanted to bid on it. That car belonged with Nico. So she bought it for seven hundred thousand, chiming in over the phone on the auction, taking the top bid away from her own father.

And then Nico came home, told her the good news about the high bid, and informed her she'd be getting the check in two days. Saying simply, "It belongs to you."

He had such a generous nature. She was feeling all warm and gooey toward him until he took off his long-sleeve Exotic and Classic Restorations shirt for bed that night, revealing a long, thin scratch with dried blood across his beautiful bicep.

"What happened?" she asked in alarm. A closer look revealed a deeper cut on one end. And then she realized this wasn't the T-shirt he'd left in this morning. It was the same logo work shirt, but long-sleeved.

He glanced down at his arm. "It's nothing. I don't even need a Band-Aid."

"You do so need a Band-Aid and antiseptic too." She grabbed his arm and stared at the cut that veered off above the elbow. How could he not have mentioned this? They'd had a normal dinner and several hours together talking and watching TV. "Why were you hiding this?"

"I wasn't hiding it."

"But you changed shirts before you came home."

He lifted one shoulder up and down. "My T-shirt got a little blood on it, so I changed. I had a spare shirt in the car."

She wondered how much blood there'd have to be before he'd mention it. "Do you even have antiseptic?"

He rolled his eyes. "Yes, in the medicine cabinet."

"Come on." She gestured for him to follow her to the bathroom. "Did you get this from working on a car?"

"No." He pulled the antiseptic and Band-Aids out of the medicine cabinet, and she took them. First she carefully cleaned off the cut with a wet washcloth. Then she dried it and applied the antiseptic. He didn't flinch once.

Instead he leered at her. "What a pretty nurse."

"What happened?" She got out the biggest bandage for the deepest part of the cut and peeled off the wrapper.

"I guess I should tell you. Just in case he tries anything else."

"Who? What?"

"Your pal Trevor threatened me with a knife in the parking lot. Slashed my tire too."

Her jaw dropped, and her hands started shaking uncontrollably. Nico had a knife pulled on him? What if it had been worse? What if he'd been…killed?

"Hey, sit down." He guided her to the closed toilet seat lid. "Don't you pass out on me, or I'll be forced to call you the worst nurse I've ever had."

He took the bandage from her and slapped it on. "It was nothing. He was drunk. Your dad promised him help becoming governor if he married you, and he was pissed that you turned him down."

"I'm going to kill him," Lily said fiercely. "And then I'm going to kill my dad. I knew he must've promised Trevor something. It didn't make sense how much he wanted to marry me." She frowned. "He kissed me once and wiped his mouth after like it was gross."

He pulled her up and gave her a smacking kiss on the lips. "His loss."

"But why did he come after you? How did he even find you?"

"Must've read about me in one of the articles about the auction. I'm glad he did. Because if he came after you, I would've had to kill him, and I don't think prison would agree with me." He grinned.

She smacked his chest. "How can you joke about this?"

"It's fine. I sent him running, tail between his legs."

She buried her head against his warm chest, and he wrapped his arms around her. "I don't know what I'd do if something happened to you."

He kissed her hair. "Nothing's going to happen to me. Promise. You're stuck with me." He turned her and smacked her ass. "Now go get naked. That's the only thing that will make me feel better after this horrifying experience."

His teasing tone calmed her immediately. She left the bathroom, Nico hot on her heels, stripping as she went. She headed for the sofa bed and squeaked when he grabbed her from behind. He nuzzled her neck and whispered in her ear, "I love you, Lil."

She melted, all the tension leaving her body. "I love you too." His sweet words got her every time.

~ ~ ~

Which was why she totally fell for it when the next day Nico put on a button-down shirt, dress pants, and Italian leather shoes and said he was taking her someplace nice for lunch. She hadn't been home in two weeks, so she only had the clothes she'd brought with her on the trip. Of course, she could've stopped back home when her dad was at work, but she'd needed a clean break for her fresh start. She put on the one dress she had, the purple wrap dress that showed off her cleavage, did her makeup, and headed out the door, blissfully ignorant of what waited for her.

When they pulled up to the Tudor-style home she

grew up in, she turned to Nico, equal parts shocked and hurt. "You tricked me!"

"I said we were going someplace nice. This is nice. C'mon. We're heading for neutral territory. The gazebo."

She didn't move.

Nico pushed a lock of hair behind her ear. "You know I would never hurt you."

Her throat got tight, and she nodded.

"I know you're not happy. Your dad called and asked me to bring you by to talk. Either way it goes, at least you've heard each other out. Then you can move on."

Her head snapped up. "He called you? When?"

"Early this morning. You were still sleeping like the dead." He gave her a slow, sexy smile. "Your boyfriend must really be wearing you out with all his sweet lovin'."

She shook her head, unable to help a small smile. "But why would he call you? What does he want?"

"It's Father's Day. Maybe he thought a little more about what it means to be a dad."

"You talked to him at the auction yesterday, didn't you?"

One corner of his mouth lifted. "I told him to man up, and he did."

She burst out laughing. She could just imagine the

tall, manly Nico telling her own tall, super-solid dad to "man up."

He grinned. "Come on."

She took a deep breath and got out of the car. Nico held her hand as they walked to the backyard. Her dad was sitting in the gazebo, head bowed, hands folded in his lap. She'd never seen him like that. Almost vulnerable looking.

She stopped at the front step of the gazebo. "Hi."

Her dad stood and looked down his nose at her. He wore his "casual" outfit—sports coat over a button-down shirt, tailored pants, and loafers. "Lily," he said in a formal tone. "Nico, can we have a moment?"

Nico inclined his head and headed to the patio in back of the house.

"Have a seat, please," her dad said, indicating the wooden bench near where he'd been sitting.

She crossed her arms. "I'll stand."

He took a seat. "All right."

She stood there, staring at him. He looked older, his shoulders stooped, bags under his eyes.

"How are you?" he asked.

"Fine."

He nodded. "Good." He pursed his lips. Sour-lemon look was back. She stifled a sigh. She just wanted to leave, she was so tired of all this—

"I refuse to accept you disowning me," he said. "I'm your father. I raised you—"

"Ha!" Lily was done with his haughty edicts. "I had a series of nannies who raised me! God forbid you let anyone stick around long enough for me to get attached. Mona hated me—"

"She did not hate you."

"Well, she certainly didn't love me. I know I look like my mother. I can just imagine how horrible it must be to see that reminder day in, day out. Of course I didn't know about Taylor as a kid. I just thought I was unlovable."

He leaped to his feet, a spry move that surprised her. "*I* love you."

Her eyes went wide. He'd never, ever said that. Even when she'd said it, he'd never returned the sentiment.

"I'm not comfortable with…emotions," he said, "like you are, but…it's Father's Day. And you're my only daughter. You're the future of the Spencers."

She let out an exasperated breath. "Why would you set me up with Trevor? You promised him money for his governor campaign. Like I was just some prize to be bartered. I mean, what the hell? What century are you living in?"

His brows drew together. "One hand washes the other. That's how politics works."

"I'm not politics! I'm your daughter!" She paced back and forth and finally stopped, pinning him with a hard glare. "I know you always wanted a son, but that doesn't give you the right to just use me and throw me away on some psycho. He pulled a knife on Nico!"

His head veered back in shock. "What? Trevor isn't violent. We've known his family his whole life. I thought he'd be the son I never had, helping you continue the Spencer legacy."

That damn Spencer legacy was like a noose around her neck. "Nico's arm was sliced by that knife. I can show you if you don't believe me. Is a psycho, politically scheming man the kind of person you want me to marry?"

His brows scrunched together. "This is very troubling. I'll look into it and be sure he doesn't bother you or Nico again."

She shook her head. "I've been a disappointment to you from the day I was born. You didn't get the heir you wanted. You were tricked and then you were stuck with me."

He stared at her. Not denying it. Why would he? It was all sickeningly true.

She turned to go.

"Wait!" he said. "You're right. I didn't get what I expected. You have to admit, though, you've been a handful. Not all of those nannies left because I fired them. Some of them quit."

Her jaw dropped. Sure, she'd run a little wild as a kid, desperate for attention, but she hadn't known she'd been that awful. He kept talking, so she turned back to hear him out.

"I didn't want you to take it personally," he said, "so I told you they weren't good enough and had to go." He stared at the ceiling and swallowed visibly. "But I can't imagine how empty my life would've been without you in it."

He blinked and sucked in a noisy breath. "I imagine as empty as these past several weeks have been."

"Dad," she said softly, "you're not disowned. Okay?"

"Oh. Good." He looked at her uncertainly. "Should we hug or something?" He held out his arms at an awkward angle and the picture he made, somehow dignified in his sport coat and awkward at the same time, melted that painful vise that had been around her heart.

She crossed to him and stepped into his arms. "Yes, we should hug."

He thumped her back in an attempt at affection. "Have you been studying for the bar?"

She pulled back and smiled. "I love you too, Dad."

"Yes, yes, good, but you didn't answer my

question."

"Ye-e-s," she said on a long-suffering sigh.

He patted her shoulder a few times. "Proud of you."

She smiled even as tears stung her eyes and turned to see Nico standing, watching them. She gestured him over. He headed toward them, and she left the gazebo and raced into his arms.

He stroked her hair. "Went okay, huh?"

She nodded. "It went okay."

"You think he'd like to join my family for our Father's Day barbecue?"

Her heart surged with love for the generous offer, even when he knew her dad was not the greatest company. "What'd I do to deserve you?" she asked.

He gave her a slow, sexy smile. "You finally got naked."

She smacked his chest playfully. "I'll ask him."

Her dad was surprised by the invitation, but gracefully accepted. "Should I dress for dinner?" he asked.

"What you've got on is fine," Nico replied. "Dinner's at six."

"Thank you," her dad said, offering his hand. "For your part in this."

Nico shook his hand. "That was all you. Nice job, *man*."

Her dad actually flushed pink. He nodded formally and retreated to the house.

CHAPTER TWENTY-ONE

Lily bit back a laugh later that day as Nico pulled on a blue T-shirt with white letters that proclaimed #1 Son.

"What is that?" she asked.

He jabbed a finger at her. "Don't laugh."

She snorted. He grabbed her. "I told you don't laugh," he said in a mock menacing voice.

"I didn't, I swear!"

"My stepmom made them for all of us. I *have* to wear it."

"Are you number one?"

He narrowed his bedroom eyes. "What do you think?"

She nodded solemnly as she bit back a smile.

"Payback, Lil. Not so much as a snicker."

She shook her head. Then she shrieked as he tickled her. And she tickled him back. Next thing she knew they were wrestling, each trying to get in a good tickle. But she was in way over her head. He had her under him, flat on her back within seconds. He straddled her and pinned her wrists above her head. Her smile dropped as his gaze turned heated. He slowly leaned down, and her lips parted on a sigh as his mouth claimed hers.

They were really late to dinner.

Which turned out just fine. They missed all the initial awkwardness of her dad showing up at his parents' house and meeting everyone. By the time they got there, his stepmom ushered them in, telling them they'd missed Gabe and Zoe, who'd already left to spend time with Zoe's dad. Vince and Sophia were traveling back from their two-week honeymoon in Mexico. Mrs. Marino told Lily it was a well-deserved vacation for them after finishing up the big Clover Park Library addition and renovation.

They followed Mrs. Marino into the living room, where her dad was sitting in Mr. Marino's brown chair.

"It reclines too," Mr. Marino said, cranking the lever. Her dad flew back to a reclined position and sat stiffly, his head slightly raised.

"Could you make it go back up?" her dad asked.

"Sure, just put your feet down and lean forward." He did, rather awkwardly.

"Happy Father's Day!" Lily exclaimed.

Mr. Marino turned and grinned. "Hey, they're

here! 'Bout time you showed up, you crazy kids!"

Lily's cheeks burned as Nico's brothers—Angel, Luke, and Jared—gave them both a smirky, knowing look from where they sat on the sofa.

Then she burst out laughing because all of his brothers had #1 Son T-shirts and Mr. Marino had a #1 Dad shirt.

"I love your shirts," she said.

They all stared at her like she was the weird one.

She got serious and nodded solemnly. "I really do."

The brothers returned to watching the pregame for the Red Sox on TV. Nico chuckled softly and crooned in her ear, "Payback."

She shivered.

Nico sat on the floor, leaning back against the sofa, and pulled her down to sit between his legs.

"You a Sox fan?" Mr. Marino asked her dad.

"I don't really follow baseball," her dad replied.

Lily stifled a laugh. Her dad liked golf, tennis, and polo, in that order.

Mr. Marino put a hand on her dad's shoulder. "You are now." He turned. "Angel, go see if I have an extra cap in my closet."

Her dad held up a hand. "That's not necessary."

"You'll like it," Mr. Marino said.

A few moments later, Angel returned with a beat-up Red Sox cap and handed it to his dad.

"There it is. Thanks." Mr. Marino slapped it on her dad's head. It was too small and perched high up on his gray hair. He gestured to the cap. "You can adjust it."

Her dad took off the cap and adjusted the back, slowly putting it back on.

Mr. Marino grinned. "We'll catch a game up at Fenway. Make a day of it." He turned to his sons. "Right, guys?"

"Yeah," they said in a chorus of deep, masculine tones.

Her dad sucked a sour lemon, and she feared he'd say something rude, but he finally said, "Thank you for the kind invitation." Which was his polite no.

"Good, that settles it," Mr. Marino said. "Beer?"

Nico nuzzled into her neck. "See how well we all get along?" he whispered in her ear. "Just wait until after dessert when we play the traditional Marino-Reynolds football game."

She giggled and whispered over her shoulder, "I'm taking pictures of that."

~ ~ ~

Two days later, Nico came home to find the Mustang Boss 429e sitting in his driveway.

"Lily!" he hollered, taking the steps to their apartment two at a time.

She appeared on the landing wearing a sexy low-cut T-shirt and a miniskirt. He was real glad she'd gotten more of her stuff from home. He loved all the skin. "Do you like your present?" she asked.

He smacked his forehead. Then he met her at the top of the stairs, grabbed her, and hugged her. "I can't believe you."

She grinned. "Come on. Let's go for a ride."

She handed him the keys. He shook his head and followed her back down the steps. "You were the mysterious high bidder over the phone?"

"Yup!"

He unlocked the driver's side door, and Lily appeared at his side. "Maybe I could drive," she said with a smile.

He stiffened. It was a stick shift in a car worth seven hundred thousand dollars. "Well…"

"Kidding! You should see your face."

He grabbed her and pinned her against the car for a hot and heavy kiss, lifting her leg so he could grind into her. Long moments later, he pulled away. She looked dazed, cheeks flushed, lips parted, halfway between surprise and lust.

"You should see *your* face," he said.

She shook her head, a bemused smile on that sweet face, and got in the passenger side.

He slipped into the driver's side and turned to her.

"Why would you do this?"

"This car was meant for you." She held up a finger. "And you have to accept my gift."

He cradled her cheek, moved beyond words, and kissed her tenderly. Things got heated quickly after their earlier kiss, and he slid his hands under her shirt, gliding up her soft skin to caress her breasts.

"Lil," he said in her ear, "all I want is you."

"I'm afraid you're getting a lot more," she said, unzipping him.

He hissed out a breath because a moment later her hand was fully around him. She licked her lips.

"Not here," he said. "This car is worth a fortune."

She slowly leaned down. Those plump pink lips with the bow at the top inching closer. "I'll take good care of it," she purred. "And you."

She took him fully in her lush mouth. He closed his eyes and dropped his head back, giving her full control. There was nothing like that mouth on him. He wished he could hold out, but she was a demanding temptress that took everything and left him dry. He exploded an embarrassingly short time later.

She tucked him back in and rezipped, giving him a cheeky smile.

He pulled her close and kissed her, a how-did-I-get-so-lucky kiss. He couldn't speak, but he hoped it got across.

She settled back in her seat and smiled. "Okay, drive."

He gazed at her, dazed for a moment by the love he felt for the woman who snuck past his defenses and unlocked his heart. He took in a deep breath and let it out.

"That almost sounded like a happy sigh," she said.

"It was. Do you have any idea how much I love you?"

She nodded happily. "As much as I love you."

"All right then. Let's see how this bad boy takes to the open road."

He put the car in gear and thrilled to the power of the muscle car as he revved it up and let her loose.

Epilogue

Two weeks later, Lily walked hand-in-hand with Nico to meet his family at the Clover Park Fourth of July fireworks celebration. Apparently, it was a family tradition. They walked into the Clover Park High football stadium entrance, and Lily was immediately caught up in the excitement as the scent of hamburgers and hot dogs grilling wafted over her and kids ran around with glow necklaces and spinning sparklers.

"You want ice cream before we go in?" Nico asked. "Shane's Scoops is the best." He leaned down toward her ear. "And I really want to see you lick that cone."

She grinned. "I will happily lick your cone."

He groaned and squeezed her hand. They waited in line and got two chocolate ice-cream cones served up by a cheerful man with red hair.

"Hey, another ginger," Lily exclaimed, pointing at her hair. "Now I know this'll be good."

"Hey, Shane," Nico said. "This is Lily."

"Nice to meet you," Shane replied. "You want extra sprinkles just for us gingers?"

"Absolutely!"

Shane sprinkled some chocolate sprinkles on top with a shaker and handed it to her.

"Daddy!" a little girl about three years old with red hair shrieked. "Hannah licked my cone!"

"You know what to do," Shane told the girl, who promptly licked the other girl's cone.

Hannah, who looked to be about two years old, swung a fist, which her mother, pregnant and pushing a stroller with a sleeping toddler, managed to block. The mom with long brown hair in a braid shook her finger at Shane. He grinned.

Nico laughed. "Reminds me of me and my brothers. Speaking of which, come on."

They headed to the stadium and found the two rows where his family sat. Happy birthday streamers hung off the ends of the bleacher seats.

"Whose birthday is it?" Lily asked.

"Mine," Nico said.

She stared at him. "You were born on the Fourth of July? Why did I not know this?"

"Because we're too busy screwing to talk about unimportant details." He grinned. "I always loved the fireworks on my birthday. We always celebrate here."

"Why didn't you tell me? I didn't even get you a

present! This is so embarrassing."

"You can give me a present later," he said with a wicked smile.

She shook her head. "I wish I'd known."

"We've only been dating two months," he said. "I forgive you."

They settled at the end of the row next to Vince and Sophia, who looked tanned and happy from their honeymoon in Mexico. She had the seat next to Sophia and chatted with her about Mexico, which Lily had been to before, while she licked her cone, and Nico licked his, watching her.

"Hey, Nico," Vince called from Sophia's other side. "Ma made you some birthday cookies."

Mrs. Marino turned around from the row in front of them and offered them a plastic container full of crescent-shaped cookies covered in powdered sugar.

"Mmm, don't they look good," Vince said. His brothers and sisters-in-law—Luke, Jared, Gabe, Zoe, Sophia, and Angel—all looked over with smiles on their faces. "Italian wedding cookies, but good for any occasion."

"Have some," Mrs. Marino said to Lily.

"I have ice cream," Lily said. "Maybe later."

Nico took one, took a bite and held it up to her mouth. "Bite," he said.

She glanced over at his stepmom smiling

encouragingly, and took a small bite. She chewed and swallowed. "Very good, Mrs. Marino."

"It's official," Vince boomed, reaching over and taking her cone.

"Hey!" she protested.

Sophia was smiling at her. "Turn around."

She did. Nico was down on one knee in the aisle, holding up a black velvet box with a small marquis-cut diamond ring. Tears unexpectedly stung her eyes, and she blinked them back. His dad was holding his ice cream cone and his whole family was standing, pressing close at her back to watch. Luke was holding up his cell phone aimed right at them.

"Lily, I love you with all my heart. Will you marry me?" Nico asked in the sweetest proposal she'd ever heard.

"Yes!" she cried and a cheer went up as the entire Marino-Reynolds clan congratulated them. Luke was snapping pictures with his cell as he crowded in close.

And then Nico slid the ring on her finger and wrapped her up tight in his arms. His family patted their shoulders and backs, congratulating them.

She gained not only a husband, but a huge loving family that day, she realized as each brother and sister-in-law hugged her in turn and welcomed her to the family. Tears streamed down her face. Happy tears for what felt like an embarrassment of riches for someone who'd grown up so poor in the family department.

She could hardly believe her luck. "Pinch me," she told Nico.

"Can I knock you up instead?" he whispered in her ear. "Three or four times?"

She flushed, hoping no one had heard that. But she nodded happily anyway.

"I heard that," Vince said with a wink. He turned and hollered down the row. "Gabe! I think we're gonna have to move Sunday dinner to your place. He's gonna knock her up and this family's not gonna fit in Mom and Dad's dining room much longer."

Everyone laughed. Gabe gave him the thumbs-up.

"That seems fitting," Mrs. Marino said. "Clover Park's where this family began."

~ ~ ~

With Lily's permission, Nico sold the Mustang to an overseas collector for a nice profit and became full owner of his shop. He stocked electric vehicles now in addition to the classic cars to do his part for the environment and was training his staff to repair them. Lily, his wife, he loved the sound of that, showed up in the Exotic and Classic Restorations showroom pregnant in her blue dress right on time. She worked from home on Fridays and always met up with him for lunch at his shop. They shared her city apartment

Monday through Thursday while he reverse commuted back to Eastman, and shared a home in Clover Park, not far from where he grew up, over the long weekends.

He loved the way the pregnancy gave her even more curves, especially that baby bump. She'd passed the bar exam, brilliant woman that she was, and had been working very successfully on behalf of the environment for nearly a year.

He smiled again at that huge belly. She was due in a month—he'd knocked her up on their honeymoon. Score! She planned on taking a year-long maternity leave to care for their daughter before returning to part-time work. They had plenty of family around to help with childcare, which was the way they both wanted their kids to grow up, surrounded by family.

He met her halfway across the showroom and gave her his killer smile—part player, part charm, one-hundred-percent devoted husband. "Hello, Tiffany."

Her sweet pink lips curved into a small smile, and she gave him a mock slap. He grabbed her hand and pulled her back to his office for their usual afternoon hookup. Where it all began. Right here on this desk with the wrong redhead that turned out to be so, so right.

~THE END~

Thanks for reading *Rev Me Up*. I hope you enjoyed it! Look for the other books in The Clover Park Series too!

Turn the page to read an excerpt from *An Ambitious Engagement*, Luke and Kennedy's story.

AN AMBITIOUS ENGAGEMENT

KYLIE GILMORE

Financial planner Luke Reynolds has his sights on a new client, but just when he's finally secured a golf meeting with the eccentric billionaire, he's told he must win the game against some upstart competitor named Ken. Unfortunately, Ken is a beautiful woman. And she beats him. Things are about to get down and dirty.

Kennedy Ward's ambition is fueled by her father's medical bills and her four younger siblings. So when billionaire newlywed Bentley Williams assumes the bickering between her and Luke is because they're a couple, Ken assures him they're happily engaged. Next thing you know, they're invited to a weekend at his estate.

Only one of them will win this game.

And one of them will lose their heart.

AN AMBITIOUS ENGAGEMENT
EXCERPT

Luke Reynolds downshifted his dark blue Porsche 911 Carrera on the winding country road leading out to the Majestic River golf course and grumbled to himself. "The friggin' sun isn't even out yet."

He flew over a dip in the road, shaking up the car, and making him take a deep breath. He wasn't a morning person to begin with, but to be up before the crack of dawn on a Monday for a seven a.m. tee time in Connecticut, a good hour's drive from his Upper West Side Manhattan apartment, was ridiculous. The only reason he'd agreed to the ungodly hour was because his prospective client, Bentley Williams, had told him Ken Ward, Luke's competitor for the account, had already agreed to the time.

Grr...he had no idea who this upstart Ken was. He'd never heard of him before and could find literally nothing on him. Must be some kind of stealth sabotage from a rival wealth management company trying to take advantage of the newly-made billionaire Bentley. The man had unexpectedly inherited the Williams Oil fortune after his older brother died of a heart attack. He'd heard rumors that Bentley was a little eccentric, that his family had carefully made him, the younger brother, in charge of non-oil related activities. In other words, parties. That was just fine with Luke. He enjoyed a good party, especially if big spenders were there who needed some guidance in their future investments. If he scored this client, he'd finally get the promotion that would put him on the top tier of the firm's wealthiest clients. This was the big whale his boss told him he had to bring in. Just call me Ishmael. Or maybe Captain Ahab. He was a little rusty on his Melville.

A cherry red Mustang started tailgating him. He hit the brakes, annoyed, and the car got right up on his bumper. He powered down the window and hollered, "Back off, asshole!"

He glanced in the rearview mirror to see a blond woman gesturing to him to speed up.

He slowed even more. It was a no passing zone—a narrow road with no center line and plenty of blind curves.

The Mustang gunned the engine and passed him

with a roar. "It's a thirty-mile-per-hour zone, Grandpa!" the woman yelled as she passed.

He stiffened. Grandpa? He was thirty-two years old. In his fucking prime! He hit the accelerator and rode the tail of the Mustang, who sped up, dangerously fast for this stretch of road. The sun still wasn't up. He slowed. Fuck it. Let that idiot end up wrapped around a tree. Not him.

He blew out a breath and told himself to calm down. He mentally reviewed what his firm could offer Bentley. What he personally could offer in terms of access, he gave clients his personal cell number so they could always get in touch. And his prior years of experience on Wall Street, trading stocks and managing portfolios. He was more than ready for the big time.

By the time he arrived at the club's lobby, his golf bag thrown over one shoulder, he was completely composed. Bentley, his thirty-year-old potential client, greeted him with a boyish grin. He wore a blindingly yellow polo shirt with pink and green plaid Bermuda shorts and was sandwiched by two beautiful blonds. Hell, maybe when you were a billionaire, you could have two blonds at all times. Luke had a couple million stashed away, which never hurt in the woman department, though he'd never had a threesome. He didn't like to share. The taller blond wore a bright orange sundress, her wavy hair nearly reaching her waist. The shorter blond, with her hair tied back in a small ponytail, wore a white polo shirt and white shorts. He did a double take as he realized the short blond was glaring at him.

Shit. This was the woman who'd tailgated him. He hoped she didn't turn Bentley against him. He pulled his wayward thoughts back on track and reached out to shake Bentley's hand.

"Nice to meet you, Bentley, I'm Luke Reynolds."

Bentley shook his hand vigorously, which made his messy brown hair fall into his blue eyes. He tossed it away with a shake of his head. "Great to meet you too! Hope it's not too early for you. I'm an early bird by nature."

"No problem at all," Luke said smoothly. "Had a coffee on the drive in."

"Good, good," Bentley said, all early-bird smiles. "This is my wife, Candy." The taller blond smiled.

Luke shook her hand and gave her his full-on charming smile that always worked on women. "So nice to meet you, Candy."

"You too," Candy chirped. "I'm just here to watch. Bennie likes me to meet all of his business associates."

Bentley pulled Candy close. "I just can't bear to be separated from my Candy. I love being married."

"Me too, sugar bear," Candy said.

They rubbed noses and cooed at each other.

"Everyone should be married," Bentley said with a goofy smile. Considering he'd only been married six months, Luke was sure the shine would rub off soon. Though some of his brothers had found love, Luke still found the whole love thing to be more of a random event. Like getting struck by lightning. The rest of the time, marriage was motive (money), opportunity (same age, same place), and chemistry (that would fade).

The shorter blond, the tailgater who'd called him fucking Grandpa, looked at him, her expression grim. Luke decided to be the bigger person. "Sorry about earlier. I'm not much of a morning person."

"I noticed," she said with a cheeky grin that had him unexpectedly smiling back. She was actually quite beautiful when she smiled, her blue eyes lit up, sort of dancing with mischief that made him want to know what she'd do next. Her face was so feminine, with delicate cheekbones, a cute perky nose, pink lips. She had a sexy athletic body, trim and toned with perky breasts. He could just imagine palming that delicate jaw, taking—

"So you two know each other?" Bentley asked.

Luke started to shake his head no when the short blond said, "Yes."

And then, as if she knew what he'd been thinking,

she went up on tiptoe and kissed him. Her warm lips brushed over his and a jolt of raw lust gripped him. Her flowery scent washed over him as she whispered in his ear, "I'm Ken." He stiffened. She pulled back, and her lips curved into a sweet smile. "Love you."

Luke was rendered mute; a strange, foreign experience for him. He prided himself on being a smooth talker. Love? Ken was a woman? She kissed him. He wasn't sure which of those things was worse. Actually the kiss was pretty—

"Honey, don't be shy," Ken said, smiling up at him, from her five foot and change of devious woman height. "You can tell Bentley."

Luke slowly blinked. "Tell him what?"

She looped her arm through his. "That we're engaged." She beamed. "The jeweler is resizing my ring. That's why I'm not wearing it right now."

His brain finally kicked into gear, and he sucked in a breath to correct that hideous lie, but something went down the wrong pipe, and he ended up choking like crazy while Ken helpfully pounded his back.

"Wonderful!" Bentley exclaimed. "Now our little competition will have a happy ending no matter what."

"What competition?" Ken asked.

"Best score today gets my business," Bentley said with a big smile. "But now it will all stay in the family.

Awesome!"

Wait, he had to win the game? He was okay at golf, not great. He glanced at Ken. She smirked.

"You can't be serious," Luke said.

"I look forward to it," Ken said.

Bentley beamed. "Don't worry, Luke. Once you're married, you share the money. Right, Candy?"

"That's right!" Candy sang.

"Thank you," Ken said graciously. "You won't be disappointed. I've been studying your company and your current investments, and have so many—"

"Let's not talk business now," Bentley said with a dismissive wave. "Let's go hit the course."

He and Candy led the way outside. Luke grabbed Ken's arm and pulled her back out of earshot. "What the hell do you think you're doing?"

"I'm making sure he likes us."

"By lying?"

"You saw him with Candy," she hissed. "He loves being married."

"Couldn't you just pretend to be married to someone other than me?"

She slowly shook her head. "That probably would've been better. I blame your sexy smolder."

"My what?"

"You were smoldering at me, like maybe you liked what you saw." She shrugged. "Too late now."

"I was not…" He trailed off as he realized he must've been too obvious in his once-over. Still, this was crazy. He had to nail down this business and losing it in front of Bentley wasn't going to help. He glared at her, and she glared right back.

"Ken is a man's name," he spat.

"It's short for Kennedy," she said through her teeth.

"I'm sure you get that all the time. Why do you abbreviate it? You should go by Kennedy if you don't want any confusion."

Her blue eyes flashed, giving him a jolt of unwanted desire. "I should go by what I want people to call me."

"Try tailgater."

"You were the one driving like an old man."

"I was tired."

She smirked. "So are old men."

He straightened to his full six foot. "It was dark! That road had dangerous curves—" He clamped his mouth shut when he realized he'd gotten loud.

"So do I!" Candy piped up, which made Bentley throw back his head and laugh. The happy couple was by the door, waiting for him and Ken to catch up.

"You're a riot, honey!" Bentley said. He turned to Luke and Ken. "Isn't she?"

"You're a lucky man," Luke said.

"Mmm-hmm," Ken said.

Bentley beamed again. "I'm thrilled you're getting married! I've talked to a number of financial planners, and I narrowed it down to you two. But I just couldn't decide until I saw who was best at golf."

Luke's brows shot up in surprise. Bentley had narrowed it down to just them? The man had billions at his disposal, and he'd narrowed it down to Luke, who'd never had a billionaire client, and Ken, who couldn't be past twenty-five? They followed Bentley outside to the golf course that had another party of four on it. Luke had thought for sure they'd be the only ones crazy enough to take on a Monday morning seven a.m. tee time. Luke puzzled over the fact that Bentley had already narrowed it down to him and Ken as Bentley took a few practice shots on the putting green. Clearly Luke had more experience, so that should automatically give him the advantage. He took a few shots and stepped back to let Ken take a practice shot. She had a flawless, controlled swing. Dammit.

"Ready to go?" Bentley asked when they'd finished warming up.

"Ready," Luke and Ken said in unison.

Bentley signaled for a couple of caddies to join them. The young men checked out Candy surreptitiously, who preened under the attention. Bentley remained oblivious.

"Ladies first," Candy said, gesturing for Ken to take the first shot. "I'm just going to watch."

"I'll go last," Bentley announced.

Ken lined up with the ball, her hips wiggling as she adjusted her stance. Luke tried valiantly not to notice her heart-shaped ass in those snug white shorts and gave one of the caddies a good glare for doing the same. The ball arced beautifully in the air with an impressive drive, landing with what would surely be an easy approach to the green. Luke broke out in a sweat over both the game that he had a sinking feeling he was not going to win, and the fact that Bentley would soon figure out that he and Ken were not getting married. He couldn't afford to damage his reputation. In the wealth management business, results and an honest reputation were critical. And the wealthy elite were a small circle where word got around fast. He well knew only one of them was going to walk away with the money. They'd be lucky to have a job at all if Bentley thought they were screwing with him.

Bentley and Candy started sucking face.

Ken raised a brow at him. He bristled and lined up his shot, closing his eyes for a moment as he tried to visualize the end result.

"Don't fall asleep," Ken teased.

His eyes flew open. He swung hard in a drive that hooked left, landing in the small sand pit just off the green.

"Too bad, Grandpa," Ken whispered as she brushed by, her flowery scent temporarily distracting him.

"Why are you here?" he whispered, snagging her by the elbow. "You look like you just graduated college."

She leaned into him and smiled, probably for Bentley's benefit, though he was still busy stuffing his tongue down Candy's throat. Not an easy task given that Bentley was a good four inches shorter. "I graduated two years ago. I'm the hungriest at the firm, and my boss knows it. I'll do anything to nail this account."

"Even me?" he asked in a husky voice meant to scare her off.

She lifted her chin defiantly, and his gaze caught on the pulse point in her throat beating rapidly. "Whatever it takes," she whispered.

He stroked one finger over the wildly thumping pulse of her throat and felt himself go hard. Fuck. This could not be happening. He could feel himself getting sucked in by the intriguing vulnerability coupled with the ballsiness. She didn't flinch, instead she held his gaze steadily. He had the strangest Neanderthal urge to toss her over his shoulder and bring her back to his place, both to protect her and keep her for himself. Protect her from what? Him? This was insanity. He was not a Neanderthal kind of guy. He was smooth, sophisticated, cultured. He'd worked damn hard to be.

"Don't play with me," he warned.

"I play to win," she growled.

Yes, growled. He'd never been so turned on. What was wrong with him?

"My turn, lovebirds!" Bentley called before teeing off with a gorgeous swing that had his ball even closer to the hole than Ken's.

Ken leaned against his side, one arm wrapped around his waist, and the way she fit perfectly made him actually believe for one crazy moment that they were a couple.

"When I win," she said out of the corner of her mouth in a low voice meant only for his ears, "we'll both be happy about the shared business. And then you'll quietly walk away."

"Like hell."

"Thanks, sweetheart!" She pulled away and gestured toward the green. "Your turn." She smirked. "Furthest away goes next."

It hit him as he stalked toward the rough that Ken was exactly like him—fiercely ambitious, calculating, and driven.

He mentally rubbed his hands together. Let the games begin.

Get *An Ambitious Engagement* now!

Also by Kylie Gilmore

The Clover Park Series

The Clover Park STUDS Series

Acknowledgments

Thank you to my family for listening to me plot with a *yes, and*, which is how all the best improv happens. Thanks, as always, to Tessa, Pauline, Mimi, Shannon, Kim, Maura, and Jenn for all you do. Thanks to my readers' group, the Gilmore Goddesses, for cheering me on! (Join us, all reader goddesses are welcome!) And big hugs and thanks to my readers, you mean the world to me!

About the Author

Kylie Gilmore is the *USA Today* bestselling author of the Clover Park series and the Clover Park STUDS series. She writes quirky, tender romance with a solid dose of humor.

Kylie lives in New York with her family, two cats, and a nutso dog. When she's not writing, wrangling kids, or dutifully taking notes at writing conferences, you can find her flexing her muscles all the way to the high cabinet for her secret chocolate stash.

Praise for Kylie Gilmore

THE OPPOSITE OF WILD

"This book is everything a reader hopes for. Funny. Hot. Sweet."
—New York Times Bestselling Author, Mimi Jean Pamfiloff

"It's intriguing and complex while still being light hearted and truly romantic. To see a male so twisted and turned is unusual but honestly made the book all the more enjoyable."
—Harlequin Junkie

"Ms. Gilmore's writing style draws the reader in and does not let go until the very end of the story and leaves you wanting more."
—Romance Bookworm

"Every aspect of this novel touched me and left me unable to put it down. I pulled an all-nighter, staying up until after 3 am to get to the last page."
—Luv Books Galore

DAISY DOES IT ALL

"The characters in this book are downright hilarious sometimes. I mean, when you start a book off with a fake life and immediately follow it by a rejected proposal, you know that you are in for a fun ride."
—The Little Black Book Blog

"Daisy Does It All is a sweet book with a hint of sizzle. The characters are all very real and I found myself laughing along with them and also having my heart ripped in two for them."
—A is for Alpha, B is for Book

BAD TASTE IN MEN

"I gotta dig a friends to lovers story, and Ms. Gilmore's 3rd book in the Clover Park Series hits the spot. A great dash of humor, a few pinches of steam, and a whole lotta love…Gilmore has won me over with everything I've read and she's on my auto buy list…she's on my top list of new authors for 2014."

—Storm Goddess Book Reviews

"The chemistry between the two characters is so real and so intense, it will have you turning the pages into the midnight hour. Throw in a bit of comedy – a dancing cow, a sprained ankle, and a bit of jealousy and Gilmore has a recipe for great success."

—Underneath the Covers blog

KISSING SANTA

"I love that Samantha and Rico are set up by none other than their mothers. And the journey they go on is really hilarious!! I laughed out loud so many times, my kids asked me what was wrong with me."
—Amazeballs Book Addicts

"I absolutely adored this read. It was quick, funny, sexy and got me in the Christmas spirit. Samantha and Rico are a great couple that keep one another all riled up in more ways than one, and their sexual tension is super hot."
—Read, Tweet, Repeat

RESTLESS HARMONY

"Kylie's writing as usual is full of laugh out loud humor, touching moments, and heat that will make you fan yourself... If you are looking for a book that will having you laughing out loud and feeling good when you are done, this book is for you."
—Smut and Bonbons blog

"My heart broke for Gabe's past, but it soared for the understanding and love in which he got through from a family born of true love and commitment. Kylie brought the real with this one. Heartache, love, support, sexiness, and beliefs."
—Reading by the Book blog

NOT MY ROMEO

"Their sexual tension and continuous banter had me smiling. I couldn't get enough and stayed up late just to finish their story, because I had to know where it went."
—Book Junky Girls blog

"They may not have been Romeo and Juliet, but they sure made one hell of a story that kept me laughing and reading on."
—Smut and Bonbons blog

ALMOST IN LOVE

"Ms. Gilmore is an excellent storyteller, and her main characters are hard to forget, but her secondary characters are equally impressive. This is a character-driven tale inside of a sweet plot to get two nice people to fall in love and have their HEA."
—*USA Today*, Happy Ever After blog

"Forget alpha-male billionaires. The Studs will have you panting for that guy in nerdy glasses."
—New York Times Bestselling Author, Mimi Jean Pamfiloff

"I was pulled in quickly and between the fascinating characters, the witty banter, the flow of the story and the emotions I was feeling I was blown away! I loved every second."
—A Beautiful Book blog

Thanks!

Thanks for reading *Rev Me Up*. I hope you enjoyed it. Would you like to know about new releases? You can sign up for my new release email list at Eepurl.com/ KLQSX. I promise not to clog your inbox! Only new release info and some fun giveaways. You can also sign up by scanning this QR code:

I love to hear from readers! You can find me at:
kyliegilmore.com
Facebook.com/KylieGilmoreToo
Twitter @KylieGilmoreToo

If you liked Nico and Lily's story, please leave a review on your favorite retailer's website or Goodreads. Thank you!

CPSIA information can be obtained
at www.ICGtesting.com
Printed in the USA
LVHW081707050419
613131LV00016B/612/P